"Adam Tallchief, In The Flesh,"

Jillian said. "I wondered how long it would take you to find me. I've been in Amen Flats exactly one and a half days and here you are."

Adam braced himself to encounter the girl, now a woman, whose memory he had carried for years. Jillian Green had been his first love…twenty-two years ago. The memory of how she had looked then, so soft and on the brink of womanhood, had nestled in his heart for years.

But that image was overlaid by the one of her vivid hatred one year later. It still lashed at him. "I hate you, Adam Tallchief. Just wait. I'll pay you back someday."

He studied Jillian's face. He wondered if he had unconsciously compared all the women he'd known to her. Had he really hunted for a woman like her all his life? Why hadn't he known until just now how badly she'd haunted him?

Dear Reader,

Escape the winter doldrums by reading six new passionate, powerful and provocative romances from Silhouette Desire!

Start with our MAN OF THE MONTH, *The Playboy Sheikh*, the latest SONS OF THE DESERT love story by bestselling author Alexandra Sellers. Also thrilling is the second title in our yearlong continuity series DYNASTIES: THE CONNELLYS. In *Maternally Yours* by Kathie DeNosky, a pleasure-seeking tycoon falls for a soon-to-be mom.

All you readers who've requested more titles in Cait London's beloved TALLCHIEFS miniseries will delight in her smoldering *Tallchief: The Hunter*. And more great news for our loyal Desire readers—a *brand-new* five-book series featuring THE TEXAS CATTLEMAN'S CLUB, subtitled THE LAST BACHELOR, launches this month. In *The Millionaire's Pregnant Bride* by Dixie Browning, passion erupts between an oil executive and secretary who marry for the sake of her unborn child.

A single-dad surgeon meets his match in *Dr. Desirable*, the second book of Kristi Gold's MARRYING AN M.D. miniseries. And Kate Little's *Tall, Dark & Cranky* is an enchanting contemporary version of *Beauty and the Beast*.

Indulge yourself with all six of these exhilarating love stories from Silhouette Desire!

Enjoy!

Joan Marlow Golan

Joan Marlow Golan
Senior Editor, Silhouette Desire

Please address questions and book requests to:
Silhouette Reader Service
U.S.: 3010 Walden Ave., P.O. Box 1325, Buffalo, NY 14269
Canadian: P.O. Box 609, Fort Erie, Ont. L2A 5X3

Cait London

TALLCHIEF: THE HUNTER

Published by Silhouette Books

America's Publisher of Contemporary Romance

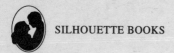 **SILHOUETTE BOOKS**

ISBN 0-373-76419-7

TALLCHIEF: THE HUNTER

Visit Silhouette at www.eHarlequin.com

Printed in U.S.A.

CAIT LONDON

lives in the Missouri Ozarks but loves to travel the Northwest's gold rush/cattle drive trails every summer. She enjoys research trips, meeting people and going to Native American dances. Ms. London is an avid reader who loves to paint, play with computers and grow herbs (particularly scented geraniums right now). She's a national bestselling and award-winning author, and she has also written historical romances under another pseudonym. Three is her lucky number; she has three daughters, and the events in her life have always been in threes. "I love writing for Silhouette," Cait says. "One of the best perks about all this hard work is the thrilling reader response and the warm, snug sense that I have given readers an enjoyable, entertaining gift."

To the Readers
I've enjoyed hearing from readers
who like the Tallchief miniseries,
and appreciate every one of you.
I hope you'll enjoy my other stories, as well.
You make all of this possible.
Thank you.

Prologue

'Twas no light matter to know that I had tossed away everything that I was bred to be, an English lady of standing. But when the night comes and my husband looks at me with those gray eyes, my heart races, for the woman within me knows what will follow.

It was not always so, for I resented his capture of me, just as his father had taken his Scots wife. 'Twas not my fault that outlaws made me take Liam while he was staked and helpless upon the ground. 'Twas not my fault that I bore and loved his son, keeping him safe in England.

Liam came for us both, claiming the child and me as his. Kidnapped and angry with the man who forced me to marry him, bringing me to this wild land, I fought what flamed inside me, the woman I had not known. Even as I fought and ran, I knew he would find me.

Perhaps even then I knew that the legend of the dove's and the hawk's feathers was true…that I would love him desperately, and that love would tear from me everything

I'd known and called safe. For in his arms, I was no longer
the well-bred lady, but a woman who would claim her due.
       —From the Journal of Elizabeth Montclair Tallchief

One

Adam Tallchief rapped just once on the door of the small home. The courtesy was more than he wanted to spare the woman inside; neither wood nor lock would keep him from her.

He glanced at snowcapped Rocky Mountains in the distance. At midmorning, they were layered with late March mist that came creeping down to lie damp upon his face. The woman inside had caused the past to leap the hundreds of miles separating this small town from another Wyoming town, the images just as bright and painful as twenty-two years ago.

Without waiting for welcome, he pushed open the door. She sat in front of the large computer screen, and turned slowly as if expecting him. The morning rain slashing against the windows wove snakelike patterns along the walls of the softly lit home. Framing her, the small house served as her office and her home. The glow of the oversize computer screen caught the rich sheen of auburn hair carelessly knotted on top of her head, leaving her face in shadows.

"Adam Tallchief, in the flesh," she said, in the soft, cultured tone he remembered. "I wondered how long it would take you to find me. You've been in Amen Flats exactly one and a half days and here you are. Elspeth Petrovna is my friend. She has no idea that we know each other and she probably mentioned my name by chance."

Her gaze skimmed the kilts and plaid he wore as she said, "It looks like you zoomed right out of her fitting to come over here and tell me off. Let's leave Elspeth and the rest of the Tallchief clan out of this, shall we? And close the door. I don't want the whole town of Amen Flats hearing this."

Adam slashed his hand through his wet hair and braced himself to encounter the girl, now a woman, whose memory he had carried for years. "Jilly" Green had been his first love... She'd been fifteen to his seventeen, and starry-eyed over the high school's prize athlete. He'd known better than to encourage her; her upscale family wouldn't like her seeing a boy "who didn't fit in." But the memory of how she had looked then, so soft and on the brink of womanhood, had nestled in his heart for years.

But that image was minimized by the one of her vivid hatred one year later. It still lashed at him—*I hate you, Adam Tallchief. I'll never forgive you. Just wait. I'll pay you back someday.*

Perhaps now was the time to exorcize Jillian from his life. He closed the door with a firm click. "Let's have this out. Now. I want to make certain you're not bent on payback and that you're not out to hurt my family."

"Protective, are you? How nice," she stated flatly, her opinion of him quivering, lashing at him from the shadows.

Adam sensed her closer study of his kilt, his family's plaid of dragon-green and the vermillion stripe to signify his Native American ancestor, Tallchief. The crackle of the fire in the old woodstove should have warmed the house, but Jillian's tone was cool and unwelcoming. "The Tall-chiefs are wonderful people…. To save any discussion with you, here're the facts—I'm leaving Amen Flats right away, just as soon as I finish this layout to the satisfaction of my customer—so don't worry about me troubling your family. Pardon me if I don't offer you coffee and cookies. I'm not likely to do that to a man who destroyed my family."

"It's Jilly Green *O'Malley* now, isn't it? The O'Malleys from the *right* side of the tracks with the nice fat pocketbook?" he asked more quietly than the simmering anger within him. At forty years old and a world traveler, Adam had learned to tether his emotions. But just seeing Jillian served up the stormy past between them. In another time, in another town ruled by her family and their friends, he'd known the greatest pain of his lifetime.

"It's *Jillian* O'Malley now," she corrected coolly. "At thirty-eight, I'm not a girl any longer. And I'm divorced."

"So I heard." Elspeth's account of her new friend noted briefly that she was still struggling with shadows, refashioning her life after a divorce.

Adam knew about surviving and struggling for a new life—Jillian's family had ripped his away when he was only eighteen. While his heart thudded heavily, and he battled the storm within him, Adam took in the furnishings of the house his sister-in-law, Michelle, had rented to Jillian. Though small and cluttered with computers and printers and books, the recently renovated old house seemed airy and light and feminine. Through a doorway he noted a dainty bedroom, magazines resting open on a patchwork quilt. Framed pictures danced across an old dresser. Highlighted beneath the lamp glow, the rich luster of real pearls threaded over a lacy doily. He knew they were her grandmother's pearls; she'd worn them to the prom.

He fought the clasp of pain delivered from the past, when he'd thought life was innocent and ahead of him, the road smooth with Jillian at his side. *Bred to wealth and class, there was little reason, except one, that she could be making her home in Amen Flats—or living in a rented cottage.*

The woman dressed in a dark green sweat suit and white workmen's socks looked little like the sleek society bride she must have been. Still, at a height just level with his shoulder and slender, Jillian wore elegance and grace as she rose and, in stockinged feet, padded to the old wood stove. "You're going to be difficult, Adam," she said in that low, smooth tone. "We could just leave it. No more said."

"Let's not leave it," Adam said tightly and, heated by his anger, shrugged free of his navy peacoat. He tossed it aside onto a small, delicate chair with tapestry cushions. He leaned back against the wall, his arms crossed, careless of the Scots plaid and the kilt he wore. He'd just come from his cousin Elspeth Tallchief Petrovna's fitting, leaving his jeans—torn by barbed wire while he was helping repair fences—to be mended. After hearing Jillian's name and her description from Elspeth, the storms that Adam had fought for years erupted and he'd had to see her.

Jillian poured hot water from the stove kettle into a cup and briskly plopped a tea bag into it. She considered the herbal brew, the line of her throat slender and exposed in the gentle light, though her face remained in the shadows. "You've always been difficult. I don't know why I should expect anything different than a full-blown attack from you."

She'd torn his heart and he resented the memories buffeting him now. As she turned to face him, he braced against the lock of those amber eyes. Though he couldn't see her face clearly just yet, he felt the cool lash of her scorn and remembered her vivid hatred of twenty-two years ago. Once more, her disdaining gaze drifted over his white dress shirt and the Tallchief plaid. Her eyes lowered slowly down to his kilt and his walking boots, damp with puddles that he'd tramped through to come to her—nothing could have kept him from her, or the battle he expected.

Adjusting to the soft light now, he noted the fine auburn arch of her brows, her cheeks trimmed of that teenage softness. Against his will, he longed for a closer view of those amber eyes. So long ago they'd been soft upon him. Then, when his world tore apart, that shaded softness had flashed into gold, hot and bright.

Her lips curved slowly, just that bit that made Adam question how often she smiled—*if* she smiled and why—and he resented the curiosity. "So Elspeth wove the Tallchief plaid for you, did she? That's like her, already fitting you into the family. March is a bit cold for kilts, isn't it?" Jillian asked, settling her hips back against the tiny kitchen's counter.

She'd torn his heart into shreds. "Worrying about my backside comes a little late, doesn't it? I was eighteen and could have used the concern while your parents and their friends were chewing on it. Why did you come here?"

"Why did *you?*" she fired back at him.

"You know why. You're renting my brother's wife's house, the one she restored. I hear you're friends with her and everyone else in Amen Flats. So you must have heard what brought me here.... I thought my brother Liam was killed as an infant—in the same wreck as our parents. He wasn't. He was claimed by a childless couple and he only recently discovered who he really was and that he had an older brother—me. He located me in Australia and I came to meet him.... And here *you* are, suddenly very chummy with everyone in town—including my relatives."

He resented the unwavering touch of her eyes, the artist seeing into the man, beyond the skin and flesh and bones.

"I don't have to say anything to you, but I don't want the Tallchiefs troubled. You're trouble, Adam. You always were and so I'll tell you what you want. But that doesn't mean you have my forgiveness for what you did."

"*Your* family and friends broke *my* aunt's heart."

"*You* killed *my* brother, or rather, put him in prison *where he died.*"

Their cut-and-slash truths were followed by the quiet ticking of a clock, the muted hum of the computer, the light crackle of fire in the old stove. Shadows danced between them, the small old house filled with warmth and feminine scents at odds with the big, humming computer, its huge, blank screen glaring at him like an eye that saw everything—the past, the pain.

"I didn't know he died." For just a moment he softened toward Jillian; he knew how much she loved Tom—enough to believe Tom's lies.

"Don't say you're sorry. I wouldn't believe you."

Her anger sizzled in the quiet room, setting off his. He didn't disguise the cool fury in his tone, spearing each word into the serene, feminine setting. "Get the facts straight. I testified at your brother's trial. He did the crime and landed in prison. He and his buddies ran a car theft and burglary ring while we were in high school."

"He died in that prison. The legal fees destroyed my parents. They had to sell everything, and then, they died of heartbreak."

After years of brooding, Adam speared the real facts at her: "Your family was wealthy. Tom and his friends didn't need to steal, but he liked the thrill. When that old woman was killed in his burglary, whether by accident or not, he was there, and I knew it. I was delivering groceries and I heard her cry, 'Tom Green—shame on you. Give me back my money.' I saw him leaving her apartment. Before that, I saw Tom and his buddies hot-wiring a high-priced sports car. I followed them to their chop shop, where they took it apart and sent the parts out for sale. I could have kept quiet about that, but not the old woman's death. She was a friend of my aunt and she nursed Aunt Sarah through some bad spells."

He closed his eyes briefly and saw the elderly woman's frail body on the floor again, blood seeping from her head wound, the kitchen cabinet too close. She'd clung to her opened and riffled purse, her apartment torn apart. When

Tom had been found, he'd had her wallet. "I would testify, and for that, the town's elite—whose sons were also involved in Tom's crimes—turned against me and my aunt. In a small town, the ruling class can bring plenty of pressure to get what they want, and they wanted to protect their sons. Bribes didn't work, and for the first time Tom and his friends had to face consequences. While waiting for the hearing, he tried to kill me before I testified. For that and other things, he didn't get off as easily as his buddies.... Why are you here, if not for revenge?" he asked bluntly.

He sensed rather than saw the probe of her eyes, tracing his features. She spoke thoughtfully. "I was surprised at how much the Tallchief family looks alike—and like you— that same night-black, thick hair of your Sioux chieftain ancestor, those gray eyes from Una, his Scots captive bride. All the rugged features are there, a bit of the arrogance, the pride, but there the resemblance ends—because I know what you are. I don't believe that my parents or their friends could have damaged Sarah or you. I don't believe that my brother led any crime ring. I've gone over this in my head for years. I think you misread the facts."

"Did I misread that Tom tried to kill me that night he was out on bond, Jillian? Did I misread the revolver in his hand? Or his threats?"

"He said he was cleaning it and intended to show it to you because you were a hunter. He wanted to make friends with you, share something in common. Yes, you misread that entire scene. Tom was angry, of course, and I'm certain his threats came out of that anger. Any person charged with a crime they didn't do is going to react."

"Oh, he reacted, all right. He was still spewing threats when I had him tied to a chair and the sheriff arrived. That incident snipped away even more of my aunt's life."

"I don't believe Tom stole anything or he was the kind of person you say he was! But he's not alive to deny it, is he?" Jillian's voice quivered with anger.

Then as though reclaiming her composure, taking time

to deal with her anger, she slowly lifted the tea bag from the cup and methodically placed it on a tiny saucer. Jillian sipped slowly, studying him before she spoke. "I met Elspeth at a weaver's fair—we share the same interest in textures and design. I created a small brochure for her work and she invited me to visit. I met her family, and she later wrote me about Liam's missing brother, Adam. You were only three when your parents and Liam, then an infant, were in that car wreck. You were battling the end of a cold and stayed with your maternal aunt. What a shock it must have been to discover that your brother was alive."

There was no expression in her tone, as though she were settling in to uncover his life's rough edges, to use them against him. Adam had been stunned to discover that his brother Liam lived and hadn't known his true identity until almost two years ago. Liam had been a widower with a small son. He had come to Amen Flats to give his boy the richness of the family's history. "You know a lot."

"I know that you ran through the inheritance your aunt left you. From the looks of you, you must have. You have no visible means of support, and you can't stay in one place long enough to hold a job. You hitched a ride here with a friendly farmer and arrived at Liam's gas station with a worn duffel bag and a backpack. That doesn't say a whole lot for your life's success, does it? You can't blame that on my family."

"Your opinion of me isn't exactly high, but it doesn't matter, does it?" Adam smiled briefly. Jillian's assumptions were wrong. He was the successful creator-owner of Sam the Truck toys and products; he simply preferred to travel lightly through life. No country or setting or community could reach into his heart long enough to capture it, and he traveled restlessly. Maybe he was hunting for something that just never appeared; maybe he was waiting for just this moment. "What did you plan to do?"

Her answer rang true, those amber eyes almost golden

as they burned through the shadows to him. "To hurt you somehow."

"Through my family."

"I didn't know how. I thought it might come to me along the way. You don't know them, Adam. You may share the same bloodline, but you don't have the heart. Yours is a cold lump, and from the looks of you that hasn't changed. I fell in love them, with Liam and Michelle's little boy, J.T., and they're expecting another baby now. I've only been here since January, but in these three months, I've come to love this family. I've quite simply changed my mind. I don't want anything to do with you. I don't want the Tallchiefs to know all this, and they're certain to see problems with you if I stay. So I'm leaving. End of story. You can go now. When I complete this project, I'm leaving. I suggest you do the same as soon as you can make your excuses."

"Now that interests me. Why should *I* leave?" He wanted to see her without the shadows between them, and moved across the room. She looked up at him, her head tilted just that bit in defiance, her anger barely shielded. He reached to turn her face to the window's soft light. The rain-snakes shadowed her fine skin, so warm and silky to the touch. She lifted her head to jerk away, and he gently tightened his hold. "I've only just discovered my missing brother and the whole Tallchief family. So again, I ask you why should I leave?"

She frowned at him. "All right. If you can step into my life, I can step into yours—and you asked for it. You're a drifter. I heard you came into town wearing pretty worn clothes. And look at those boots, the laces knotted and re-tied. I bet they've seen plenty of highway road when you were hitchhiking. You look like you haven't been to a barber in a while. You told Liam that you don't have a job right now, and you're not looking for one. My guess is that you're looking for a warm spot to settle before you move off, taking whatever you take. The Tallchiefs are a close

family. You can't use them. How long were you planning
to stay? Long enough to get money for the road? What
about your little nephew J.T.'s heart? He's terribly excited
about you arriving. He's only four, Adam, and the more he
is attached to you, the more it will hurt him when you
leave.''

J.T. had loved the present Adam had given him, a special
collector's issue of Sam the Truck with his friends. Adam
was already in love with the boy, and half in love with
Liam's wife Michelle. Just staying at their home for a day
and a night had told him that his brother was well loved.
The warmth of their love permeated their home. An expec-
tant mother, Michelle fairly glowed—a beautiful thing to
see. Liam and Adam had lost a childhood together, but as
men, they would build a solid friendship. It would be no
easy task for Adam to leave his brother's family. Jillian's
assessment of his wandering life raked at his pride; he'd
been able to keep fresh, to establish a profitable toy company while traveling.

He studied Jillian's face. That fierce, rigid, simmering
anger that ran through her tone, visible in her features, as
well. He wished his fingertips hadn't just caressed that
smooth, warm skin. He wondered if he had unconsciously
compared the women he'd known to her. Had he really
hunted for a woman like her all his life? Why hadn't he
known until just now how badly she'd haunted him?

He glanced at her left hand, locked knuckle-white to the
counter. Those fine slender fingers had once brushed his
cheek, her eyes asking him to take her—and she'd worn
his silver ring. Now they were bare. ''What happened with
your husband? The family run him off, too?''

He damned himself for slashing at her, for wanting to
know everything at once, and maybe, to just see if she
tasted the same, to kiss those luscious lips firmed now with
anger. Once they had trembled and begged him to take her
with him, to marry her. In exchange for recanting his orig-

inal story and keeping his silence, he could have had Jillian and money and the Greens' financial support.

At sixteen Jillian had been the Greens' sacrificial lamb—they'd been a family set on freeing their only son, the family's male heir valued more than his female sibling. He remembered her father's less-than-concealed offer of his daughter…a girl. A girl raised to please her family. The perfect daughter. He remembered, too, her frantic pleas. *She'd known what they wanted—what she wanted. She wanted to protect her brother, and she wanted Adam, the high school leader in scholastics and sports, the potential All-American success.*

"Stand back from me," she said, her voice low and uneven.

Her order reminded him of others issued long ago. *Leave town. Don't testify against Tom or his friends. Forget you saw anything, knew anything. It will be worth your while. But if you go ahead, you'll be sorry.*

"Am I making you nervous? Or don't you like remembering what your family did? That when I was set to testify against Tom, they and their friends controlled the town and everyone in it? How they used that power against me and Aunt Sarah? Don't you think it hurt her to see her longtime friends fear for their jobs? To move away from her on the church pew? To exclude her from their social circles? The gardening club?"

His anger built and stormed and burst then. "Aunt Sarah had a bad heart, Jilly-dear."

Adam threw her teenage name at her, a reminder that the past lay between them, raw and brooding. "Aunt Sarah raised me, all by herself, and she could have had a few more years without the pressure put on her when I testified against Tom and his friends. But she said I should do what was right for me, and never wavered from that. She died before I graduated high school."

He ran his hand across his heart, where memories of his maternal aunt Sarah ran close and warm…Sarah, a woman on her own, doing her best to raise a child that wasn't hers. She'd never complained, and loved him without restriction. "She wasn't well, but she could have lived a few more years without all that stress."

He'd never told another person that, and guilt now nagged at him. He questioned again for the thousandth time if he should have testified.

Jillian's gaze softened, searching his. "I am very sorry about Sarah. I liked her very much. I did spend some time with her at the last. She called me and asked me to come over."

"She called you? One of the Greens? Why?"

"She had her reasons." Jillian's pressed lips said she wouldn't explain further.

Adam slapped the flat of his hand on the counter. Then he turned from Jillian, closing her away from his grief. "But you didn't like her enough to do anything to help, right?"

The silence grew and throbbed, before Jillian said with quiet elegance, "We both lost people we loved. And I think we've said quite enough. It was a long time ago, and it would suit me to never see you again. Goodbye, Adam."

The sound of the rain upon the roof and against the windows hammered at the silence as Adam fought the past and the anger that had simmered for years—and the newly recognized need to see Jillian again. He ran his hand across his jaw and tried to settle the hunger in his heart for a girl who had stolen his dreams; her secret place in his heart had denied him any other woman. "What happened to O'Malley?" he asked again, needing to know more about her.

"It doesn't matter," she answered slowly from behind him.

He turned slowly, eyes narrowed upon her, ready to catch the slightest indication of what had happened. "But it does. He would have been a perfect catch for you. Just what your parents wanted—an ex-senator's son, a political career all laid out for him.''

She sighed and looked out into the rainy mist swirling in front of the window. ''You're going to gnaw on everything, aren't you? I knew you would. You were always very good at putting pieces together. You're not the captain of the debate team now, Adam.''

''This is a very private war, Jilly Green O'Malley. Your revenge against me is no small thing. I want to make certain that you don't intend to hurt my family. If gnawing on old bones clears the table, then I will.''

''If you need that to leave me alone, then I'll give you the answer—Kevin and I simply grew apart.''

The odd tremor in her tone drew him on. Was that a shudder passing over her body? Or just the shadows of the past stirring between them? And why should he want to hold her close and keep her safe as he had years ago?

Disturbed by that thought, Adam moved to her computer, and one light touch on the mouse brought it to life. He noted the advertisement she was creating on the screen. The vivid red cabbage roses surrounding a sleek, black perfume bottle contrasted the gray day outside. The logo was that of an exclusive perfume designer, Silver Tallchief, who, Adam remembered, was married to Nick Palladin. ''I thought you were getting a business degree.''

''Please leave,'' she whispered so softly that the sound of the rain on the roof and windows almost drowned out her words. She pushed a shaky, delicate hand against her face, and when it came away, her cheek gleamed damply.

He desperately wanted to hold her against him, to protect her. Adam mocked his emotions with a quick, grim smile. He hadn't come so far in all these twenty-two years, he decided darkly. Jillian could still take his breath away with a look, with a word.

He slowly pulled on his jacket, sorting through his thoughts. ''You came hunting me, Jilly, and now that you've found me, you want to run. It doesn't work that way. Not until I'm satisfied. We'll talk again.''

''I'll be gone before that.''

''Then I'll come after you.'' A memory slithered through the shadows, nagging at him. With his back to her, he asked, ''Do you still have the ring I gave you?''

''I can't remember,'' she said. Her careless tone implied that the ring was long tossed away. ''Probably not.''

He nodded and pushed himself into the cold, gray mist that was safer than his emotions concerning Jillian.

After Adam had gone, Jillian stood very still, battered by the furious past moments.

At six-feet four inches, Adam Tallchief, dressed in his Scottish ancestral plaid and kilt was not an easy image to push away. He had stood in the doorway, carrying the swirling mist of cold rain with him. It had beaded his wind-whipped, shaggy hair and gleamed upon his dark jacket. The white-frilled dress shirt had contrasted his hard, tanned face and, bound by the Tallchief broach, the plaid had added to the breadth of his shoulders. The kilt had accentuated his masculinity, those strong legs braced apart in a fighter's stance. Add his stormy temper to the mix and he was unforgettable, tearing into the quiet shadows of her home, slashing at them as surely as he would have held a sword in battle. In shadows, all angles and planes, his rugged face had caught the dim, soothing light in which she preferred to work. The color of steel, his deep-set eyes had flashed fiercely at her, ready to defend his family. The tight line of his mouth had said he'd do what he had to do to protect his family and that he wouldn't forget the past.

Nor could she. Jillian sucked in air and straightened her shoulders; she fought for control, for the peace she'd had before he'd torn into her home. She hadn't expected to see Adam, hadn't expected the forceful impact of him—like a Scottish laird swooping down from his castle to waylay any intruders into his realm. His scents curled disturbingly around her—the angry male fresh from the rain and her past. Even the leaves of her large philodendron seemed to quiver, stroked by his anger.

She smoothed the leaves, running cool beneath her fingertips, a contrast to her seething emotions. *Her brother died in prison because of Adam Tallchief's testimony; her parents had died of heartbreak. She'd come for revenge, to somehow take as Adam had taken.*

Jillian's racing heart, the emotions she fought to keep under control, settled slightly. The reality was that she couldn't bear to harm the Tallchiefs. She'd fallen in love with the family who had struggled to stay together. Left orphaned when the eldest was only eighteen, the five Tallchief children had used their Scottish ancestor's journals to "add glue to the mix." They'd hunted for Una's lost dowry and reclaimed each piece with its legend. After only two full months, Jillian loved the family that had grown with each marriage. "Now how could I possibly try to destroy that?" she stated harshly to the shadows. "Well, Adam Tallchief certainly ruined my peace and harmony, just like he always did."

She impatiently rubbed the headache brewing in her temples. "He's got me talking to myself. I don't want to think about Adam. I simply want to finish this contract and leave."

Determined to forget Adam's fierce expression, those slashing gray eyes, Jillian firmly sat at her computer. It hummed and waited to be fed, but Jillian's mind had locked on Adam. He brought with him the sense of storm-tossed seas, of faraway exotic places, and a fresh painful lash of the cruel past.

She stared at the cabbage roses on the screen and couldn't remember what she had planned, arranging the many layers of the graphic advertising collage. An image of Adam stalked through her mind, hacking at her creativity; she saw him as an eighteen-year-old boy, determined to testify against her brother, refusing both her offer to run away with him and the marriage she knew her parents would support. At fifteen, she'd adored him. A "mature" seventeen-year-old, he'd dismissed her. At sixteen, her feelings for him hadn't changed and, for just that month before her world came apart, Adam Tallchief was her boyfriend, the high school senior dating a lowly sophomore.

Jillian turned to the windows, seeing past the rain, back to when Adam's tender kisses turned to hot, hungry ones, his tall lean body shaking with desire against hers. He'd touched her gently, with reverence and never improperly, and filled with dreams, she'd known he would be her husband, her lover.

She slowly opened a desk drawer and removed a small box. The ring he'd given her the night of the prom was tarnished, just as was the image of how she had later flung it at him. The small silver circle had bounced off his cheek and had fallen untended to the floor. She remembered the pain in those gray eyes, the stiffening of his tall, rawboned body, the clenching of his fists at his sides as she had slashed at him, "I hate you, Adam. If you don't want me, all I'm asking is that you don't testify against Tom."

"You don't believe me," he'd stated softly, as if she'd just knocked the wind out of him with a physical blow.

"Absolutely not. My brother is not a thief, and I believe him. He says he didn't do any of those things," she'd hurled at him.

Now, with the silence quivering after Adam's departure from her home, Jillian settled into her thoughts. The silver ring on the tip of her finger was not costly, and represented just one dreamy month with Adam Tallchief. He'd been so tender and protective, and she'd dated him, despite her parents' objections—that had been her first rebellion.

Looking back, she suspected that Kevin O'Malley was a handy fix-up for her parents' shaky finances, and a rebound for her broken heart. Unfortunately, Adam's tender treatment hadn't prepared her for the rough marital sex that Kevin preferred. With a five-year marriage ending in divorce, Jillian believed that she was frigid, as he had claimed.

Twenty-two years ago she'd been a girl, loving Adam. Now she was a divorced, successful sales executive turned graphic artist, and she hated him. But not enough to hurt the Tallchiefs. Resting in the box was the reason Adam's aunt Sarah had called her: two feathers—one each from a dove and a hawk. "Give these to him when he's not fighting to survive," Sarah had said. The old woman's trembling fingers had smoothed the feathers lovingly, as though they'd reminded her of someone long ago, dear to her heart. Jillian had not been able to refuse the dying woman's request to safeguard the feathers for Adam.

Jillian touched the two feathers bound by an old ribbon, strange things for Adam's aunt to give her for safekeeping. Adam had loved Sarah and she had loved him in return.

"He's a drifter and he's probably lost everything of her, or sold it. I will send them to him after I leave. Or to Elspeth, if he's gone by then." Jillian turned to the computer screen again, critically studying her layout for Silver's advertisement. She had just gotten started as a freelance graphic artist, her experience as a sales executive useful. The Silver account was the largest she'd had; she hoped it would lead into even bigger ones as she created a niche in advertising. She had a knack for photography and for editing the images she produced; they were unique, not "canned"—shots produced by a photography mill. The cabbage roses had been photographed last summer in a perfect sunset to bring out the lush color and contrast of the shadows.

The different layers of the images could be arranged and the photography altered to her creative notions. Life was like that—arranged in different layers, some bright and good, and others shadowed like the petals of the roses. Though the photographs could be changed to her liking, her past with Adam remained painful. Still, their future was uncertain, open to manipulation, like the layouts. Jillian turned away from her computer screen. In another time, another place, she just might have revenge.

Two

Adam knocked at Elspeth's door and nodded as she opened it to him, her son balanced on her hip. The farmhouse was quiet around her, a contrast to his churning emotions. Locked in his thoughts, he dismissed her lifted eyebrows, that mocking curve to her lips.

"Thanks for the use of the pickup truck. I'm sorry I left the fitting. I forgot something in town." He served her the lame excuse while his mind coursed through the slash-slash meeting with Jillian. He had no right to bring his anger into Elspeth's home, filled with life and happiness.

"Come in. Whatever you've lost will come back to you. It's only waiting for the right time to be born as it should be." Her quiet gray eyes searched his face as the shy toddler on her hip toyed with the heavy black braid crossing her shoulder.

Caught by her tone, and the furious moment that had just passed with Jillian, Adam entered Elspeth's home. She couldn't know of his past with Jillian. Yet the certainty was there, as though she sensed the future. He took in the scents of baking bread, of children and the farmhouse warmed by Elspeth's work. His gaze slid to the large room where Elspeth wove in the quiet hours. The enormous, ancient, wooden loom threaded with the Tallchief plaid had belonged to Una, a Scots bondwoman captured by the chieftain. A quilting rack, much like the one his brother's wife used, hugged the ceiling, waiting until it was needed. In the air hung the same serenity that Adam had noticed at Jillian's, the feminine peace he had shredded with his anger.

Jillian's eyes were still as gold as he remembered, still brilliant and burning with her fury....

"You've been hunting a long time, Adam," Elspeth said as he hovered between clashing with Jillian and the serenity of the Petrovna home. "Perhaps it's time for you."

"The kilt is a bit breezy up the backside in cold weather," he said in an effort to waylay the uneasiness prowling through him. He sensed that soon he would be coming to Elspeth for answers that had eluded him for years. *She couldn't know his past and yet somehow—*

"So my brothers say. Would you like to stay and have lunch with us?" She nuzzled the black hair of her son, a close replica of Adam's nephew, J.T., but with the curling hair of his father, Alek Petrovna. The boy hugged the shiny new Sam the Truck that Adam had given him, a plastic, rounded model designed for a toddler. "Your jeans are mended, but it will soon be nap time and we can talk without curious little ears. But then, you're not ready yet, and you're set on another course, aren't you?"

Surprised that she could read him so easily, Adam shot her a wary look. There it was, that nagging suspicion that Elspeth's gray eyes saw beyond what she knew for fact. Her smile changed into warm laughter. "I grew up in a houseful of brothers, and my husband wears that same brooding look when he's stalking a new problem. Stay or leave, it's your choice. But it's better to stand and fight."

Slightly uncomfortable now, Adam shook his head. He was certain that Elspeth referred to something other than her hospitality. "Liam expects me at the station. It seems he needs to iron out another dent that Michelle gifted to his favorite truck."

"I'm glad you're staying for a while," Liam said later in the garage. He ran a loving hand over the dent his wife had just placed in his treasured pickup truck. Michelle's determination to drive a stick shift was both endearing and dangerous. "You think that by hiring Jillian as a graphic designer for your Sam the Truck ads you can keep her here, too? Without her knowing who you really are?"

The spacious garage was neat, a collection of little-boy toys resting on the cot J.T. used when he came to the gas station. Adam picked up a tiny metal truck marked by a Sam the Truck logo. "I'm not done with her. I don't want anyone else to know that I own the company...or that Jilly—Jillian O'Malley and I have a past."

"Be careful. Revenge can boomerang in a bad way. Elspeth will know. She may not know the particulars, but she'll know more than what you think. They say she has the seer talents inherited from her Scots ancestor, and the shaman insight from Tallchief's side. When their parents were killed in a convenience store robbery, Elspeth took the place of her mother. She has Una's journals, and Elizabeth Montclair's. Elizabeth was an Englishwoman who married Una's and Tallchief's son, Liam—my namesake. After our parents died in that car wreck, the woman who raised me insisted on keeping the name Liam. I brought my son here after my first wife died, after I discovered my real identity, because I wanted J.T. to have more than I had. And then I met Michelle. I have a feeling that Elspeth knew or sensed what lay ahead of me. And what was inside me, though I kept to myself back then."

"We've lost a lifetime together. I had no idea you were alive. Aunt Sarah moved from Iota to take a better paying job in New Pony, and I grew up there. Now I've got a brother, a sister-in-law, a nephew and another one on the way. I've much to learn about the rest of our Tallchief family. You're comfortable here, with them?''

Liam's smile was warm. ''I'm home. 'Aye,' as they say, I'm home. I'm a lucky man. You've traveled the world. If you're thinking of settling down, we'd be glad to have you around.''

Adam lifted a wary eyebrow and smiled. ''A built-in baby-sitter? Uncle Adam?''

Liam chuckled, a rich, full sound. ''We've got plenty of built-in baby-sitters. But you need a few of J.T.'s mind-blowing questions and a little drool on your shoulder and diaper changing to get the real texture of life.''

''I've never felt the call of drool and diapers.'' Or maybe he had… Maybe, in just that one month when he was eighteen he had dreamed of Jillian and himself with a bright new future. Before he'd seen her brother running from the dead woman's apartment. Before he'd discovered Tom's auto theft ring, and seen it in action. Before honor had demanded that he testify, despite the pressure of the families in New Pony.

Liam studied Adam with those cool gray eyes so much like his own. ''You're brooding about what happened in New Pony…how you testified because you had to, and how the town threatened you and made life difficult for Aunt Sarah. I wonder why the Tallchiefs didn't recognize your name on the news media and come to help. New Pony is only a few hundred miles away. They would have—''

''The case was shut up. Power in a small town can do more than it has a right to. Jobs were threatened. Records were sealed and pressure placed on key people to keep silent.''

Adam tossed the toy truck onto his nephew's cot. He'd left New Pony as soon as he'd graduated, glad to be away from the pain the town had caused. And Jillian. He'd been so young and certain that she would believe him—but she hadn't.

Liam was silent, then asked quietly, "Have you ever wondered why Sarah never said our parents were on their way to see the Tallchiefs, here in Amen Flats? It seems logical that our mother—her sister—might have told her since she was keeping you."

Adam had asked himself the same question many times through the years. Sarah had steadfastly ignored his questions about his parents' destination. Parents usually left telephone numbers and information when they left children with a sitter; according to Sarah, she had expected a call that never came—only news of the parents' and Liam's deaths arrived, and soon after Sarah had taken a new job away from Iota.

The absence of that telephone call from his parents had sliced away thirty-six years that could never be recovered. Sarah and he wouldn't have had to struggle alone—the Tallchiefs would have helped....

"I've thought about it. But Sarah didn't know, and it seemed too painful to her every time I pressed. She loved our mother deeply. Apparently, it was a pop-up chance to visit long-lost relatives and they were going to call when they arrived. They never called. There wasn't much of an inheritance from Aunt Sarah. She was ill for a long time and medical expenses were high. But our parents' will provided for both of us and it's been gathering interest all these years. With your share of the inheritance, you should be able to build a nice house on that ranch you just bought... By the way, Jillian thinks I'm a professional drifter, and maybe I am. With a laptop and modems and infrequent business meetings, I've managed to build Sam the Truck into a nice little company."

Adam ran his thumb over the new dent in Liam's beloved pickup truck. "I've got to find a place to work. I'm developing a new line of accessories and need to take care of regular business decisions."

Liam grinned and finished, "J.T. has almost the entire line of plastic cups and plates and friends of Sam the Truck. If he knew you were Sam's creator, he'd be a preschool star."

"I ordered him the complete highway set. I hope you don't mind."

"J.T. has been wanting that." Liam studied Adam. "I know how difficult it is to fit into a family, to get the rhythm and the warmth of it, to be comfortable. I was overwhelmed at first, but there is nothing like family, Adam. There's an old cabin on the ranch we bought and you can find some quiet there to work, if you want. We're just finishing the house plans now and will start building soon. You're going to have a rancher for a brother."

Liam glanced at Adam's mobile telephone and laptop batteries charging on a workbench. "You have what you need to work, I guess, and the old wood cookstove keeps it warm. You're welcome to the cabin, or staying with us. I've got an idea that the Tallchief family—and it's a big one—is giving us time to reacquaint, but they'll be having a dinner at the old house soon for a gathering of the clan. Later, when you're more comfortable with them, you'll be expected in full plaid and kilt—my wife finds me quite adorable in them."

Adam grinned. "'Adorable.' You look just like me. A little younger, a little less worn, but the same."

Liam lightly punched Adam's shoulder, an affectionate play he'd learned from the Tallchief brothers. "Aye, we're a handsome pair we are. Swaggering, manly—"

His grin widened when Adam gave him a sturdy shoulder shove, but not enough to hurt. He'd seen brothers jostling in fun, and a thread of sorrow ran through him—he and Liam had missed so much. "Lay off. I'll take you up on that offer of the cabin. Where is it?"

Liam's gray eyes had a definite gleam. "Well, now. That will cost you. Please use my pickup truck. It's safer in your hands than in my wife's. The way she strips the gears tears at my heart. By the way, Michelle is all set to pamper you. In fact, all the Tallchief women are probably warming up their ovens now to spoil you. Calum's wife, Talia, just may enlist you into her plays.''

His hand rested on Adam's shoulder, then slid to take Adam's in a handshake. They were men now, their boyhood together torn from them. It would take time for the bond that had already started to grow. "I'll keep your secret, Adam. Do what you have to do. I've found a home here that I've never had. I hope you'll find peace here, too.''

"Not with Jillian in the neighborhood,'' Adam said brooding darkly. "I'm not finished with her.''

Liam chuckled and grinned. "Maybe you won't ever be,'' he teased.

"Lay off. That was a long time ago.''

Just then, four-year-old J.T. burst into the station, carrying story books. At the door, Michelle's smile was happy as the boy leaped into his father's arms. "Daddy! Uncle Adam! Guess what? A big box came on a truck today, and someone gave me the whole Sam the Truck set of storybooks and gas station and railroad crossing signs and Irma the Flatbed and Mr. Mechanic and— Daddy, the whole Sam the Truck Highway Happy Set is at our house.''

Adam leaned back against the counter, enjoying the little boy's delight. He'd worked hard to build Sam the Truck products, but the real joy wasn't in financial returns—it was in moments such as this, a little boy's or girl's excitement. The toys were designed to give lessons in safety, in crossing railroad tracks and watching street signs. The books demonstrated kindness to others and were inspired by his childhood with Aunt Sarah. She'd often used his old toy trucks to demonstrate all the life lessons that Adam now used in his products.

"Liam, you could have told me,'' Michelle said, coming to kiss her husband. "That was a pretty extravagant gift from you—but appreciated, as you can see.''

"A friend gave me a good discount," Liam returned lightly, and winked at Adam.

By noon, Adam sat on top of the cabin's shingled roof, repairing it. He was used to "making do" in primitive conditions; he enjoyed the physical work while he thought of Jillian and the simmering past between them. Then through the rain and mist, trucks came prowling, stopping in front of the isolated cabin. He hadn't expected his relatives so soon, yet they stood, emerging from the mist and staring up at him. Their features, so like his own, stunned him.

"I'm Birk Tallchief," said the man strapping on a carpenter's tool belt. "These are my brothers, Duncan the Defender and Calum the Cool." He motioned to three men not bearing the Tallchief black hair and gray eyes, but just as tall. "These are my brothers-in-law. The curly haired one is Alek, Elspeth's husband, and he's Talia's brother. That's Joel Palladin, Fiona's husband. That's his brother Nick, married to a cousin, Silver. Their brother Rafe married Demi, another Tallchief cousin, and they'll be along when they can."

"Nice to meet you. I'd invite you in for dinner, but a sandwich from the grocery store's deli isn't going to serve all of you." Adam studied the Tallchiefs' features. Jillian had been right; they were a match to him—tall, lean, with dark complexions complementing their black hair and gray eyes. The Palladins were a different matter, with brown wavy hair and one looking like the other. According to Elspeth, the five Tallchief children had fought to stay together, but the three Palladins had had a rougher course— their father had tried to rob the convenience store and instead had killed the Tallchiefs' parents, who had stopped for pizza for their hungry brood. With their father in prison, the Palladins had managed to keep their honor, despite a few minor teenage scrapes.

"Elspeth said you'd be staying," Duncan said as he began helping Calum unload boards from the back of the truck. "Some of the flooring needs replacing before the furniture arrives. It's an odd assortment—just old things we're not using—but it should serve. We'll have plenty of food soon enough, but the orders were to get a proper floor laid and to sturdy up the old porch."

"I'm not staying long. It might not be worth your time and effort."

"It is. We've got orders from our wives to make you comfortable, to see that you've got a dry roof over your head and a warm house in which to sleep. Liam said you were planning to use the sleeping bag and camping gear you borrowed from him, but you'll have a lot better than that before tonight."

"I'll pay for what I need," Adam stated more firmly. Borrowing from his brother was one thing, but taking the time and money of others wasn't for him. He was uncomfortable with charity, and Jillian's opinion of him as a drifter living off others had rankled.

Duncan had been only eighteen when he'd taken on the responsibility of his younger siblings, of holding the family together. He understood perfectly. "Aye, you've got the Tallchief pride."

Birk slapped a hand on Duncan's shoulder and called up to Adam. "You've got to think of the women, man. They love nothing more than to coddle a long-lost relative. You'll make heroes of us just by letting us slap a few boards on that place and hammer some nails."

Adam had intended to keep his distance, to not get involved with his relatives, but from the look of it, he was already being swept into their midst. "I'm not married, so I wouldn't know. I appreciate your offer, but surely you've got better ways to spend your time."

Calum watched Adam descend the old wooden ladder, then shook his hand. "You can stay with any of us, you know. Sybil and Duncan have plenty of room in the old house where we were raised. Lacey and Birk have remodeled that old bordello, and Talia and I would be glad to

have you. Elspeth hasn't put her offer into the ring, and
she usually has a reason for what she does. I'd say she
already has you pegged as a man who calls his own life
without much help from others.''

''At one time, I could have used it. I was too young for
what was handed me. I couldn't protect someone I loved.
I made it, but she didn't.''

Duncan turned slowly to him. ''Had we known, you
would have had our support. Liam said you had a hard time
of it. We were lucky to have the love of the community
here in Amen Flats. Elspeth took mother's place at four-
teen, and I did my best...so did the others. It was hardest
on Fiona as the youngest, because she wasn't meant to
follow rules. And she knew she had to, or we'd be separated.''

He glanced at Joel and at Alek, who were already hauling
a power saw setup into the old cabin. Birk was starting a
generator on the back of his truck, preparing to hook up
the power to the saw. ''Looks like we're in business,'' Birk
said.

Unused to family milling around him, Adam tried to
catch his breath. ''I can manage. I'm used to camping—''

Nick Palladin removed his Western hat and ran his hand
through his dark brown wavy hair. ''You wouldn't send us
back to our women, defeated, would you? We were sent
here on a mission to build and bond. You have no idea
what they can do once they set their minds to it. We'll be
home with the babies, and they'll be roofing and sawing
and probably talking about a quilt design as they work.''

''It's not an easy thing to take when I haven't paid—''

''Oh, you'll pay. We share fencing work and herding and
whatever else needs done, so it's no free ride for you, chum.
We'd be glad to have the help.''

Adam nodded, understanding the give and take of bar-
tering, and pushed his pride aside. They thought he was a
homeless drifter, riding hard times, and they wanted to
help. By refusing, he'd hurt them. ''Fair enough.''

"Hey, Adam," Alek called as he carried a bundle of shingles to the cabin. "Thanks for fixing the fence. I hear you looked 'sweet' in the kilt and plaid my wife made you."

"Sweeter than you, my dear," Adam returned with a grin. Though a loner, he somehow at once felt at ease with the men.

Alek took the light taunt and passed it back with a cheeky grin. "Ah, but you've yet to see my knees. Scarred a bit, maybe, but still a confection to delight female eyes."

"You're full of it," Birk noted with a light elbow jab to Alek's ribs. "Get to work. You, too, Adam. If I don't come back with a good report to my wife, Lacey, she'll be out here remodeling. She's good with a saw and hammer, and that's the reason I fell in love with her."

"What I want to know, dear hearts, is how full of it you would be if your wives were here?" Adam asked.

The rest of the men grinned and Adam smiled. It appeared that Liam and he had quite the family, and one worth defending against any revenge Jillian might plan, despite her assurance that she wouldn't.

But he wasn't letting her go too soon, not before he'd had the answers he sought. Why had she lingered in his heart all these years? Why had just the sight of her tossed him back into life?

Jillian sat in her SUV, studying the small cabin. Settled amid the cold, drizzling rain, the cabin windows seemed to glow gold through the night. It would have been a welcoming sight, if Adam Tallchief hadn't been inside. The words they'd flung at each other scraped the silence inside her vehicle.

Your family and friends broke my aunt's heart.

You killed my brother—or rather, put him in prison where he died.

They were harsh words, lying deep and smoldering within their hearts and only torn free by stormy tempers.

The grief Adam had caused her parents had hurried their deaths.

She smoothed the small box she intended to give him along with a piece of her mind. Jillian had kept the feathers and brooded about her revenge, how she would track him down and make him pay.

Payback wouldn't work now, not amid his newly discovered relatives. She didn't want them to know that he'd lied, testifying and causing the death of her brother.

From their meeting this morning, Jillian knew that Adam's resentment had not lessened. Jillian had kept his silver ring. But she wouldn't have Adam thinking it meant anything—that the brief young love between them still warmed her heart.

Bracing herself for another raw, spare-no-feelings encounter, this time on her terms, Jillian got out of her vehicle and tramped through the mud puddles. She rounded the twin heaps of roofing debris and odd lengths of lumber and found more on the porch. Pieces of worn linoleum lay heaped nearby. One glance told her that old wood mixed with new. The sturdy rug in front of the door was slightly frayed but serviceable, and Jillian scraped her boots, taking the time to brace herself just that bit before knocking. She tugged up the collar of her stylish full-length raincoat, and breathed deeply, calming herself before the storm that was Adam Tallchief. In that instant she saw him again in the plaid and kilts of dragon-green cut with stripes of vermillion. All male, defiant, angry, he was no gentle picture.

Adam opened the door, dressed only in jeans. Clearly fresh from bathing and scented of soap, he impatiently swept the towel over his hair, around his throat and over his chest. His hair gleamed in the kerosene lamplight, standing out in shaggy peaks as he brushed it back with one hand and tossed the towel aside with the other. The rich, warming light behind him stroked the width of his bare shoulders and ran down his sides to his jeans. The raw visual impact of Adam's hard, muscle-packed body was enough to stun Jillian, and she realized she was holding her breath—years ago he'd had the same height, but his body hadn't filled out to the whipcord leanness of this man's.

A large circular pattern of scars danced low on his side, while a scar slashed across his upper arm. A smaller one ran a thin pale line across his dark chest.

Adam considered her a moment and pointed to his side. "I tried to save the world for a time. A shark gave me this, off the coast of Australia."

He pointed to his arm and to his chest. "Rhino poachers in Africa and a harpoon from an illegal whaler.... I've got a few others. Some seen, some not. But you already know about those. What brings you here?"

"Here," she said, after pasting herself together and pushing on with her mission. "Sarah thought this was important and said it belonged to you. She was dying and said there would come a time when you were less troubled. She wanted you to have this. I said I'd see that you got it. I only did it for her—not you. Here," she repeated, shoving the box at him.

A muscle contracted on Adam's jaw, and in the shadows, those cool gray eyes narrowed, almost sleepily. But the tension springing from him wrapped around her, tight and burning. His fingers brushed hers as he took the box, tossing it to the table behind him. "Afraid to come in and visit a while, Jilly-dear?" Adam asked in a low tone that challenged. "Or would you like a spot of tea and cookies?" he asked over-politely, reminding her that her earlier hospitality had been lacking.

"I'm not at all afraid of a visit with you, Adam, but I didn't come for tea—I came to tell you what I think of you. I wasn't quite done while you were telling me off earlier," she said airily, refusing to be intimidated. When Adam opened the door wider, bowed slightly and swept his hand in front of him in an enter-my-abode gesture, Jillian swept by him.

"I expected you within an hour of our meeting. It took you long enough to work up the courage to come calling."

"I don't need courage to face someone like you. I was working."

The old wood cookstove's oven door was open, clearly a source of heat. In front of it, the soapy water in a round galvanized tub said he'd been taking his bath. Various odd pots and cooking utensils ranged across the shelves near the stove, a metal dishpan for washing dishes sat on a crude counter. The single room smelled of new lumber, a bubbling stew on the stove and freshly bathed male. The odd collection of furniture ranged from an old rocking chair, big enough to be comfortable for a man of Adam's size, and a large, sturdy, simple oak bed with a patchwork quilt.

Adam's few clothes were neatly stacked on top of an antique dresser, his backpack hung from a peg on the wall. A braided rug made a circle in the center of the small room, and on the wooden table rested a thick file amid a triple-layer chocolate cake and two apple pies. A couple of pairs of socks, two T-shirts and a flannel shirt hung from a rope near the stove, and damp jeans had been tossed over the back of a chair.

"You travel light, don't you? There's no more here than what you can stuff in a duffel bag. No attachments, no paycheck, no obligations."

"Lead on, Jilly. Slash right down to the bloody bone, why don't you?" Adam crossed his arms in front of his chest and looked at her. "Well? From the expression on your face, you came to give me a piece of your mind. You can start anytime."

"I'm concerned," she began after a pulsebeat of trying to dismiss how her heart was racing, how the sight of him, the scent of him, stirred her. "I was at the grocery store and the gossip is that the Tallchief family has taken you under its wing. That the whole clan came out here today to work on this place and to make you comfortable. Michelle called, and though she was disappointed that you wouldn't be staying with Liam and her, she thought that you might be here awhile.''

Jillian met his shielded gaze and crossed her arms. ''You're not, are you?''

''Are you?'' The question-for-an-answer came flying back.

''I told you I was leaving as soon as I finished the project.''

''How soon will that be?''

''Under a week to finish, if it's acceptable to the client. If not, I have to either return the money or start all over, and that will take some time. I'm just getting started in this career, so it's not likely I'll return the money. You can't do this, Adam. Think of Liam and J.T.''

He breathed heavily, those steely, cold eyes narrowed now, a vein in his throat throbbing beneath his tanned skin. ''Can't do what?''

''You know what. You can't let them provide for you. You've got to make something of yourself. You've got to get a steady job.''

''So now you're telling me how to live my life again, is that it?''

She leaped over his anger, thrusting at him, determined to make her point. ''I care for the Tallchiefs. Elspeth has become a dear friend. You can't just dip into their lives and take and live off them, then go on your merry way.''

His hand raised and Jillian didn't expect the finger that stroked between her brows. ''You said the same before. Still defending people from me, Jilly? Maybe my relatives would have believed me all those years ago. Maybe with their help, you might have read the truth in the newspapers or heard it from the radio. Then you might have been forced to believe me.''

Jillian pushed down her temper. ''It's a waste of time to argue with you.''

She ripped out her checkbook, slapped it open on the

wooden table and scribbled a hefty figure. "Here, this is road money, so you can be on your way."

"Money isn't the answer, Jilly." Adam dismissed the check on the table and his low voice said his temper rippled at the offer. "But then, raised as you were, maybe you don't understand the difference. You always did what your parents wanted, didn't you? Even offering yourself to save Tom."

She faced him, careless of her fists balled against her sides. He'd humiliated her all those years ago. Was it her pride that nicked at her now? Or the truth? "Leave my parents and my brother out of this. You've done enough damage."

This time, Adam's finger stroked his jaw as he considered her. "Not quite. I'd be blind not to recognize the reaction you had when you saw me just now. Those amber eyes almost swallowed me. What's the matter, Jilly? No love life?"

While Jillian considered a proper flattening retort, Adam did the worst thing—he leaned down to brush her lips lightly. "To see if you taste the same," he whispered as she tried to catch her breath.

She shivered and fought the surge of fear curling around her, choking her.

Adam frowned, pulling back. "You're shaking, and you've just paled. You're not angry now, Jillian—you're afraid. Of me?"

Locked in panic, Jillian fought the nightmare of her husband's sexual attacks. Unable to move, she could only stare at Adam. "I—I'm not afraid of you."

The frown became a scowl. "We may be cutting and slashing at each other because of the past, but I'd never lift a hand to hurt you, Jillian."

She tried to speak, to make light of her reaction, and couldn't. She could only stare at Adam, images and pain swirling around her, swallowing her.

"Jillian, it was only a little kiss," Adam said very softly. "Sit down."

Instead, panic threw her to the door. She opened it and ran through the rain to her SUV. She slammed the door, locked it, and sat shaking, her fists locked onto the steering wheel.

When she managed to look at the cabin, Adam was standing in the doorway, his arms crossed. Then, as if he could not stand more of her, he stepped inside and closed the door.

Jillian forced herself to calm, to breathe evenly, before she started the SUV. After reaching her rented home, she tried to work, but the creative design she'd seen in her mind escaped her. Images of Adam had pushed it away.

In her anger, she'd written the check for almost her entire bank balance. She'd left a high-paying job as an executive in sales to study graphic design. The leap from knowing what attracted a buyer's attention to visually creating it had been easy enough. With classes and equipment to start her fledgling business, she'd drained her resources. The check to Adam left her finances stripped. But after her commission on the Silver perfume advertisement, she would have enough to leave town. Adam was a drifter; with her money in his pocket, he'd be gone before her. *That was what she wanted, wasn't it?*

It would be hours before she slept, because the brush of Adam's lips was warm and safe, just as it had been years ago.

How could he taste the same? Wild and free and mysterious, as if he needed to be caught and treated gently? As if she needed to fly with him into that wild, free world?

Three

Why had fear filled Jillian's golden eyes? Why had she been so terrified by a simple brush of his lips? Did she hate him so? What had happened to her?

Two hours after Jillian left his house, Adam paced the confines of the cabin, shoving his hand through his hair. He hadn't wanted to know anything about New Pony news, and Tom's death had surprised him. Using his laptop, Adam had researched newspaper archives to find the deaths of her parents and Tom. Tom's obituary lacked the prison information and the cause of his death. There had been an auction to sell off the Greens' furniture and their home. Through time, the other members of Tom's teenage gang had carried on their family traditions as adults in New Pony, becoming "respectable."

Jillian must have been shattered. She thought little of him, except to hate him for her brother's imprisonment and his death there. Yet that didn't justify the leap of fear within her, that shivering, the paling of her face. Or did it?

The newspaper's archived account of her wedding to Kevin O'Malley had been detailed. The perfect wedding. But the bride's expression hadn't exactly been glowing; she'd looked stunned.

Adam shook his head, his research answering his questions, but raising others. Once he'd protected another woman, one who had been abused by her boyfriend. Her body had tightened at the slightest touch meant to help or to comfort. Jillian's expression was of that same, tight fear. He remembered Kevin O'Malley as a college student and two years older than himself. Kevin was rich, spoiled, a party boy and not exactly sensitive. The son of an ex-senator, his parents had designated his future in politics.

Jillian would have been a perfect match with her quiet elegance, that intelligence, and would have improved his status in society and politics. His family's money would have been needed by the Greens when they'd hit financial problems. They'd probably had to pay more than legal fees—Adam remembered the judge's order, "Make financial restitution for the damage... Repayment is due for vandalism, theft and stolen vehicles."

The good things in life had probably been handed to Kevin, including Jillian.

Whatever had happened to Jillian, her scars were unseen. Adam rubbed his hand over his side, where the scars of a shark attack remained; in comparison, those he'd gotten from testifying against Tom were much worse and slower to heal. He still carried the pain of being unable to protect his failing aunt, and he held his grief deep inside.

Adam shook his head; he didn't want to think of Jillian in the hands of O'Malley. He didn't want to think of Jillian at all—or did he?

Passing the table, he opened the box from his aunt Sarah. The feathers, one white and soft, the other, the bold color of a hawk, were bound by a worn red ribbon. Adam's fingertip stroked the soft dove's feather, and in doing so, moved it within the ribbon. Now the feathers spooned, the hawk's curving to the dove's, almost sensuously, protectively, as though they had been fitted for life.

Strange that his aunt hadn't given the feathers to him earlier. She'd sometimes had odd turns to her, questions she hadn't wanted to answer. Adam frowned slightly, remembering Liam's question about their parents' destination. Sarah had firmly stated that she hadn't known where they were going, that they were to call upon arrival. When Adam had questioned her, she'd become upset and he'd stopped, sensitive to her grief.

Yet, by asking Jillian to help deliver the feathers, she'd given him something of a father he couldn't really remember. Though Adam had paid the rent on the safe-deposit box his aunt had left, he didn't want to open it again. After her death, he'd been eager to get away from New Pony. He'd respected her wishes and buried her in Iota, next to her sister—his mother—and family. Then as she'd wished, he'd collected her brooches and family Bible with other mementos and tossed them into the locked box in the First National Iota Bank, careless of what else was inside. *Sarah....*

Adam put the lid on the box with the feathers, just as he had sealed away his past. Now Jillian had brought it back.

Still locked in his thoughts of Jillian and her puzzling fear of him, he flipped open the file Liam had given him. Sybil, Duncan's wife, had prepared a genealogical chart of his family. Una Fearghus, Scots bondwoman, had married the chieftain who had captured her, Tallchief. Their son, Liam, had married Elizabeth Montclair, an Englishwoman, and their son, Ewan, had gone to Alaska. He married a Frenchwoman, Josette Benoit. Their three children had returned to the American West, and Liam's father, Jamie, had married Tina Olson.

Adam's eyes read the words, and his mind understood them, but contrasting images of Jillian, the girl and the woman, wouldn't let his thoughts stay on course. Adam slapped the file closed and picked up Jillian's check, study-

ing the large, perfect, feminine script. He tossed the check
back to the table and jammed his hands into his back pockets.

With the crackle of the fire in the old woodstove, Adam
considered his choices. He could burn the check, make his
excuses, and be on his way. He could forget meeting Jillian
again. Or he could take Elspeth's recommendation to
"stand and fight."

He reopened the box with the feathers and studied them,
nestled together within the bounds of the old ribbon. Perhaps Jillian and he were like that, tied by the past, until it
could be put aside and they each went on their way.

Or not. Adam stroked the white dove's feather, feminine
beside the rakish appearance of the hawk's. Maybe he
wanted to know what haunted her, why she feared that
slight brush of his lips. Maybe he wanted to tear her apart
for believing Tom's lies instead of the truth.

He tapped the check with a fingertip. It wasn't much, but
it was all he had of Jillian. He slid it inside the file folder
for safekeeping.

Whatever ran between Jillian and himself, Adam wanted
to examine it and he needed more time. He was considering
his next step, when Elspeth called his mobile telephone
number. "Tomorrow we're having a family gathering at
the old homestead, where Duncan and Sybil live now.
We're expecting you. Be prepared to eat."

"Should I bring anything?" Adam asked, and realized
that this was his first family gathering. His maternal grand-
parents were deceased and Aunt Sarah had been his only
relative.

"Aye. Bring your heart and a good set of nerves for the
children who will be sizing you up to Liam and their un-
cles. You'll have tiny fingers in your ears and probably be
wearing drool on your shoulder before the night is over,"
she teased softly. "You're definitely a fresh candidate for
diaper changing."

"Aye," he replied, returning the tease with a smile. "If you're trying to frighten me off, it isn't working."

When they said goodbye, Adam shook his head. This "family gathering" summons was his first, and he was set to enjoy it. Maybe the years of traveling had left him hungering for a home and the sound of women and children. Maybe there was more of Sam the Truck in Adam, reflecting the constant travel; but Adam lacked Sam the Truck's friends. Perhaps that was why Adam enjoyed creating the stories and the products, a family all his own.

He dialed Sam the Truck's corporate offices and left a message for an overnight shipment of the toys. It would be a heartwarming scene he intended to remember, the Tallchief children happily playing with his creations.

The next day, a drift of light snow swirled around Liam's pickup truck as Adam drove to the Tallchief Cattle Ranch. The chill of the late afternoon foretold a cold night; the smoke rising from the sprawling rock and wood home was inviting. Soaring in the distance was rugged, snow-covered Tallchief Mountain and the nearby lake looked black and cold, whitecaps whipped by the late March winds.

Adam parked beside other cars and pickups in front of the home where the five Tallchiefs—Duncan, Calum, Birk, Fiona and Elspeth—had fought to stay together after their parents were killed. "Stand and fight," Elspeth had said, and Adam wondered if he were meant to stay in one place for long. He already knew how to fight—survival in New Pony after he'd testified against the teenage gang had been no easy affair.

A quick survey of the various parked vehicles told him that Jillian hadn't arrived. Just as well, Adam brooded silently; he wasn't finished with her or certain of controlling the temper she could still rake from him. He didn't want to make a bad impression on the family Liam treasured, as did he.

In a last-minute fancy, and proud of Elspeth's gift, Adam

had slung the Tallchief plaid around his shoulders. The wind tugged at it now. Collecting the big sack filled with a variety of Sam the Truck models—from the elaborate with a doll driver down to the plastic with rounded edges for toddlers—Adam stepped from the truck. He hunched his peacoat collar up against the wind that smelled fresh and clean, scented of pine and smoke. After a day of clearing up the rubble in front of the cabin, hauling the old linoleum away and burning the wooden rubble, Adam had given himself to the mind-clearing task of chopping wood. Sam's brand new friend Nancy the Flatbed Hauler needed a spiffy ad campaign launch with a new storybook already brewing in Adam's mind. He could almost see Nancy on the plastic highway with her other friends—Tracy the Pickup Truck and Eddie the Railroad Crossing Warning with his red light and his long, movable, black-and-white arm.

In the distance, veiled by the light snow, cattle grazed upon several huge round bales of hay. To the other side and sheltered from the elements by a rock bluff, the thick coats of a small sheep herd almost blended with the snow. "Aye," he whispered to the wind, lifting his face to it. Amen Flats was a place for belonging—if you weren't the footloose kind.

Elspeth opened the door before he knocked, a toddler balanced on her hip, this time not her own, but with eyes just as gray and hair as black. A long sleek braid coursed down her red sweater. "Aye. It is a good home to come to when the heart is weary. The house has been added to and changed a bit, but holds a treasure of memories of dark times and of good. Ah, you're wearing the plaid. That's good, wearing of the colors when you come home. I only wish I could talk my brothers into doing the same more often."

"Da?" the toddler ventured, holding out his chubby arms to Adam.

The warmth of Elspeth's knowing welcome, the life and

scents inside the house, and the boy, unafraid of strangers, curled around Adam's heart. He rummaged through the sack of toys and found a squeaking, rounded plastic truck, just right for a teething toddler, whose delighted squeal caught the attention of the other children.

"You've only got one heartbeat to take off that coat before they get you," Elspeth whispered as Alek came to place an arm around her. "Come in and meet the rest of your family. You're rested, I hope?"

Alek, editor of Amen Flats's newspaper, tugged his wife's long braid and grinned. "You'd better be. There's no rest amid this crew. Fetch this, carry that, get more wood, change the diapers—uh," he grunted as Elspeth's elbow lightly sought his ribs.

She placed the toddler on the floor and as he made his way across the room, Birk caught and tickled him before lifting him into his arms. The scent of baking bread and love curled invitingly around Adam as he studied the huge room, filled with a family he'd never known.

Elspeth took the plaid and hung it by the peacoat Adam handed her. She waited patiently while his gaze skimmed the room. Near the huge rock fireplace hung a spear draped with the Tallchief plaid, the barn wood burned with the Tallchief Cattle Ranch brand, a stick man and mountain. In a warm corner, an old wooden cradle with a sleeping baby was being rocked by a loving hand.

The expressions of tenderness and warmth struck Adam as he noted their faces, most with coloring matching his own gray eyes and black hair. He nodded to Liam with Michelle sitting upon his lap.

Elspeth made sweeping introductions while children played on the floor and bounced on knees and slept in loving arms. There was Nick, holding hands with his Silver, Duncan with his red-haired wife, the genealogist and the antique huntress, Sybil. Calum stroked his wife Talia's long blond hair, and Birk toyed with his petite wife's, Lacey, curling black hair. Rafe Palladin had arrived with his Demi, and Joel's arms were around his wife, Fiona Tallchief Palladin.

The love in the room stunned Adam full-force. As did the look of instant acceptance, as though he had always been one of them.

A beautiful girl, just college-age, came sauntering to him. The firelight played over her long red hair. The younger boy at her side, clearly adored her. "I'm Emily, Sybil and Duncan's daughter."

"I'm Cody Palladin, Joel and Fiona's son," the boy said promptly.

She slid him a cool, older-woman look, then J.T. pushed through their legs. J.T. locked both arms around Adam's leg. "He's mine! This is my uncle Adam. He's my daddy's brother and he's been all over the world. He's going to come to preschool with me and tell all about sharks and lions and castles and sunken treasures. He's going to find what he's lost and what he's hunting—right here with us— that's what my daddy says."

When Adam glanced at Liam, his brother was suddenly finding the rough beams of the ceiling very interesting.

Emily's hand on J.T.'s head was gentle but firm with warning. "I have something to say," she announced clearly to the room with the elegance of royalty. She placed her hand on Adam's shoulder. "I claim thee for my Black Knight," she stated dramatically. "'Twas not long ago that I claimed Duncan, Birk and Calum. The others came later, but mean just as much. When I was young, they took away my fear, and I belonged. I trust you with my safety and my family, oh, Black Knight of the Tallchiefs. In return, I grant you my everlasting friendship and love—with one condition. Do not try to fix me up with a boyfriend."

"I swear I will leave your love life untouched. The decisions are yours."

"The bargain is sealed, Black Knight." She stood on tiptoe to kiss his cheek, and took the opportunity to peer inside his sack. "I don't suppose there is anything for me in there."

"Emily!" Sybil admonished.

Adam solemnly gave Emily the special collector's Sam the Truck. "I hold your trust dear, m'lady. I shall fight to keep all that is dear to you with my last breath. Please take this humble treasure as my pledge."

She beamed up at him and a steady blush crept up her cheeks. "You're okay, I guess."

Fascinated with Emily's happy expression, Cody straightened. "I pledge to do whatever he said," he announced boldly.

Adam handed the sack to Cody. "I don't suppose you'd help pass these out, would you? And take one for yourself?"

"Will I? *Will I?* I love Sam the Truck," Cody said, forgetting his attempt to impress the elegant, beautiful Emily. He took the sack and hurried to sit in the center of the braided rug, the children clamoring to sit around him.

While Cody meticulously chose the appropriate model for the age of the children, Elspeth stood on tiptoe to kiss Adam's cheek. She patted it gently as a knock sounded on the front door. "You've got their hearts already, now you'd better tend your own."

Jillian entered and glanced at Adam coolly; her smile to the rest of the Tallchief family was filled with warmth. She glanced at the children playing on the floor, the Sam the Truck models grasped tightly in their hands. "Did I miss the party?"

"Not at all. Jillian O'Malley, meet Adam Tallchief, our wandering cousin. He's staying with us for a while and brought the toys. Emily has already claimed him as a Black Knight." Elspeth took the covered dish Jillian carried, giving it to Alek with a look that said, "Place it on the table."

"J.T. seemed pleased enough with his Sam the Truck set and I thought it might make a good impression."

Jillian's narrowed look took in his comfortable, clean,

but worn gray sweater, jeans and loafers. Her expression said she doubted his ability to pay for the toys. "If a costly one."

"An expense I can afford—I've come into a bit of money recently," he said to remind her that they'd tangled twice and he was more than ready for a third helping. Adam noted the furious lash of Jillian's gaze, though her lips were smiling. He noted again the way she stiffened when he moved close. "Let me take your coat."

He couldn't resist a tug at that silky hair, a boyish urge to tease her, too intense to be denied.

Her eyes narrowed and a slight flush rose in her cheeks, a reflection of the anger she was fighting to control. "I hear you travel the world, never settling for long, Mr. Tallchief. Are you planning to stay long here?"

"Adam," he corrected while children's shouts of delight brought their parents all down to the floor to play. His eyes locked with Jillian's. "As long as it takes."

She smiled coldly and moved away into the family playing on the floor. Every instinct in Adam told him to go after her—more, it told him to pick her up and carry her out of the house, to taste those lips once again. When he was able to tear his eyes away, Elspeth's cool gray ones were waiting. "Our ancestor, Tallchief, was a hunter. I'd say it runs in the family," she said as though understanding he would seek Jillian out wherever she went.

The dinner set at the huge table was not a quiet affair with parents feeding children, the talk a blend of crops, family and Jillian's work for Silver's new ad campaign. Seated across from Adam, Jillian avoided looking at him. Then, in clearing the table, passing back and forth from the kitchen, she leaned close. "So you're already spending my money and none of it on tickets out of here. I thought that was our agreement. You can't stay and let this family provide for you. And you'd better not take the pickup truck that Liam loaned you when you go. Michelle says that truck

is almost another baby to him. She's quite fond of the hours
they've spent together beneath it.''

"I don't remember any agreement between you and me,
Jilly-dear,'' he whispered back, and let his gaze wander
appreciatively down her classic black sweater and slacks.
The pearl strand was creamy and elegant and genuine, just
like Jillian, bred for perfection, for the ideal life. But now
there were curves filling out the cloth and the flash in her
eyes spoke of anger—simmering and withheld, but real anger, just the same. "You've changed a bit since you were
young and sweet.''

Jillian sniffed, turned up her nose and hurried away to
collect another stack of dishes. Adam crossed his arms and
leaned back against the wall, waiting for her to pass by him
and into the kitchen. She shot him a hot, narrowed-eyed
glare. "They'll see through you soon enough, Adam.
They'll try to put you to work and you'll be stuck for answers and you'll be gone, just when they are counting on
you.''

"Hmm. Work. Now there's a new thought,'' he returned
lazily, thinking of all the lumber he'd cut and cleared, the
horses he'd broken, the harvesting of crops, the ships he'd
sailed and unloaded, the buildings he'd helped construct.
More often than not, he'd dragged home at night, too tired
to eat or sleep before the next day started it all over again.
Even now, with Sam's success, he preferred hard, exhaust-
ing physical labor to sleepless nights and mourning Sarah.

She pushed the stack of dishes at him. "The other men
are helping. You could do the same. You ate enough for
two.''

"So you noticed? I didn't know I interested you so
much.'' Adam's taunt belied his discomfort. He'd rarely
been in family settings and was at odds with the duties of
a guest.

"You don't. For them, you've got to do something with
your life. So they won't have a shirttail relative always
needing money. You've got to be respectable,'' she whis-

pered at him, then glanced down at J.T. who was looking up at the adults curiously.

"I'm working on it. Don't worry, I won't cash the check locally. No one will know you wrote one to me."

"You must have. Those toys are expensive."

"I like toys, and especially Sam the Truck," J.T. stated firmly below the brewing, yet controlled argument.

Adam handed the dishes back to her and picked up his nephew. "She's pretty, isn't she, J.T.?"

"Aye," J.T. murmured, and studied Jillian seriously with his gray eyes. He looped an arm around Adam's shoulders. "But she's lonely. There's a boy at preschool with that same look. His mom just went to heaven. His dad works all the time."

"Mmm. Maybe there is a truck in the sack for him. Let's go see," Adam said, and carried the boy into the living room. He suspected that J.T.'s observation was correct, but now was not the time to question Jillian. He intended to make more time with her, to wipe away the memories that had haunted him for years.

Why should she care about Adam Tallchief? Why would one look at him, standing with a child on his hip, a child that matched his gray eyes and glossy black hair, stun her? Why would the image of Adam, preparing to leave the Tallchiefs, their plaid slung over his peacoat excite her?

Maybe as an artist, she was susceptible to images. Maybe as a woman, the biological tug to have a child of her own went straight to her womb. Maybe Adam Tallchief didn't have her thinking straight; he brought the past and her pain with him, intent upon examining his own wounds.

His face was hard now, not a boy's, and those sleepy, careless looks he gave her didn't fool her. The need for revenge coursed through him, the same as hers coursed through her. But she wouldn't allow hers to erupt, to make the Tallchiefs uncomfortable.

Jillian shoved open the door to her house and moved

through the soft shadows. She preferred her comfortable, rented home to the bright revealing light. She stripped off her coat and lit a small arrangement of candles, intent upon having a quiet glass of wine to settle her nerves after the encounter with Adam.

She poured sangria into a cup and kicked off her shoes. They were practical now, black leather flats and not dress heels as she once wore. She'd once had the perfect set of wineglasses, Irish crystal, and now she used a plain white cup purchased at a discount store. But then, she wasn't hosting Kevin's dinner parties as he wangled for a bid in an election, was she? She sipped the wine and thought how well the cup served her needs as a single woman, tossing away the past—but she couldn't, could she? Not with Adam prowling through her mind, her dreams.

She cupped the stoneware in one palm and circled the rim with her fingertip, enjoying the cool, smooth surface. Life should be the same, without any unexpected chips.

Adam Tallchief was a big chip in the smooth life she wanted. He brought the past and anger with him, and storming out of her were emotions she didn't want to unravel. She had to push him away, to forget him, to make him seem as inconsequential as— She turned at a noise, and found Adam sitting at her desk, sock-covered feet propped upon it, his hands locked behind his head.

The cup she'd been admiring tumbled from her shaking fingers and crashed upon the floor. "You!"

He rose slowly and came to kneel in front of her, picking up the pieces of the cup and dabbing away the drops of wine with a cloth. He stood, placed the pieces and the cloth in the sink and, while Jillian was considering her next move, asked softly, "What did O'Malley do to you?"

What hadn't he done? she thought wildly, intimidated by the size of Adam standing too close. He lifted his hand slowly, carefully, and as she watched, her throat dry, he stroked her hair with the lightest touch. A touch that hurled

her back twenty-two years to when she was a girl adoring
him, her heart skipping with romantic expectations—

"You may not believe this, Jillian, but I am sorry about
Tom's death. I know how much you loved him. I'm sorry
about your parents, too."

Horrible scenes of her drunken parents arguing swirled
around Jillian. "They lost everything. They were humiliated."

"And you were the golden offering to O'Malley."

"They wanted me to be taken care of." Even as she
defended her parents, a cold chill swept over Jillian, the
reality of truth. "We'd lost everything by then, thanks to
you. There were legal expenses and money paid to reim-
burse those who had been robbed—not that Tom did it, but
my parents paid the bills just the same. I wanted to drop
out of college because of the expenses. I wanted to work
and help them, but they wouldn't have it. All I have left is
my grandmother's pearls."

You owe us. The harsh echo from the past dried her
throat even now. Her parents had wanted to sell the pearls,
too. Her grandmother was the only person who had really
loved her, and Jillian had lied then, saying she'd lost them.
Her parents wouldn't let her drop out of college, because
she needed that degree to catch an up-and-coming husband.
"So now you know everything, the damage you've done.
Are you happy?"

"Not quite. Do you ever wonder what would have happened between us if that fracas with Tom hadn't erupted?"
he asked softly and eased a strand of her hair behind her
ear.

"No," she lied, and turned away to look at the flickering
candles.

That prowling fingertip circled her ear. His breath
brushed her skin as he whispered, "Do you ever wonder
how it would have been to—"

"No," she lied again, and realized she'd spoken too urgently, too harshly. "Why are you here?"

He pulled a square folded paper from his jeans' pocket and tossed it to the countertop. "Your check. I didn't spend your money on those toys. I gave them to the children because I enjoy watching them play."

She turned to him then, his face lit by the candles. She saw more than she wanted in his eyes, almost silver now, narrowed upon her. That fear danced in her again and she swallowed, leaning away from him. "If you had a family, you'd have to stay in one place and take a regular job with benefits. The cost would have been too great. And that's why you never married. Right, Adam?"

"I made my choices. I saw you at the family gathering. You like cuddling babies and playing with the children too much to not have children of your own. No little ones for you and dear Kevin?" he returned too softly.

"It didn't happen." She shook her head and shivered, repulsed by the thought of Kevin's touch. Then she looked down at her hand, locked to the countertop, and found Adam's big warm one covering it. It felt too solid and safe. She slid her hand away.

"Why are you here?" she repeated, and realized that fear, memories, and something else danced along her nerves. She didn't want to think of that tense, electrified feeling Adam could evoke in her.

"To let you know that there is no reason to jump when I'm near, or to pale as if I'd hurt you. I do not want my brother and relatives thinking I terrorize women. It isn't good for the image," he stated firmly.

She stared at him. "'Good for the image'? What image? You're a down-on-your-luck drifter, so far as I can see."

He tilted his head, and despite the warning-smoke color of his eyes, said quietly, "I have my good points, you know."

"I don't want to hear what you think of yourself."

"No, but you're ready to tell me your thoughts, aren't you? Well, let me tell you mine, about you. You edge away from the slightest accidental touch of a man. I saw proof of that tonight. You'd better keep that under control, or they'll wonder and ask and try to help. You don't want anyone helping you, do you, Jillian? You want to pass out advice to others, though.''

"I've heard enough. Get out."

"I'm not done. If you avoid talking to me as you tried tonight, they'll sense something runs between us. Unless you want that examined, try a little harder to be at ease with me, will you?''

"I don't owe you anything, Adam."

"Oh, yes, you do, you little witch. You've deliberately come back into my life and now that you're here, you're not ready to take the consequences.''

"Such as?'' she invited, challenging him.

"This,'' he said softly before he lowered his lips to hers.

Caught before the fear could tear at her, Jillian could only stand still, held by the merest light, warm brush of his lips. In it was beauty and tenderness and hope, long shriveled and forgotten. Sadness welled up inside her, and came trailing down as tears upon her cheeks.

When she was able to pull back into her shields, Adam had gone and she was in for a long, restless night.

That night, while he was certain that Jillian stewed about him in her home, Adam called his friend and most trusted business manager, Steve Morris. Adam intended to keep Jillian in Amen Flats until he could resolve how he felt about her. On one level, she stirred ugly memories of the past; on another level, he wanted to hold her either in safety or as a man needs a woman. And just maybe, he felt guilty about her hardships.

Nancy, the new toy flatbed hauler, would need advertising layouts. Jillian O'Malley was a perfect candidate. Steve would contact her with the offer that needed immediate attention; using the name "Sam" and electronic mail, Adam would work with her, just as he'd worked with other artists.

He shrugged as a splash of guilt hit him. Opportunistic? Yes, but then, as Elspeth said, the Tallchiefs had hunting blood. If he had to use a Sam contract as bait, then he would.

He thought about their past and pushed it away, separating it from the moment when her lips had lifted just that bit to his. The incredible sweetness of that moment had torn at him.

Or maybe it was desire. Adam shook his head. He was a meticulous, controlled man, and even as a youth, he'd only had one sexual relationship—a girl he'd hoped to marry. She'd wanted someone else, and even then, he was amazed at how little it touched him, while parting with Jillian had nearly torn him apart.

Adam toyed with the two feathers, the dove's and the hawk's. Lying together, they seemed feminine and masculine, yin and yang. Why had they meant so much to Sarah? What had she wanted him to know?

What were the answers to the questions she had avoided? Were the feathers part of that?

He stroked the soft, white dove feather and thought of Jillian. Why did the need to know her as a woman nag at him? Had time softened the almost-forgotten fury inside him?

Why had he wanted to hold her close and keep her safe?

Four

The next afternoon Jillian couldn't wait to tell Elspeth her good news. She hurried into the bright sunlight and almost leaped into her SUV. Her exciting morning call had pushed away the sleepless night, haunted by Adam and his gentle touches, that last light kiss.

She'd overslept, then awakened in a tangle of sheets to the business offer. Sam the Truck manufacturers had contacted her to do advertising layouts, and from the moment of the offer, she couldn't concentrate on the almost-finished layout for Silver. The owner and creator was a very private man and he would be contacting her by electronic mail to discuss his ideas. If the business arrangements were suitable, she would sign a contract that would bring in better money, and would take her to bigger clients.

Jillian's hands clenched the steering wheel as she drove toward the Petrovna ranch, her mind a flurry of creative ideas and the sight of the Tallchief family all on the floor, playing with Sam the Trucks.

She'd have to finish the Silver ad first, and she'd have to— In a corner of a sprawling field, she noted Adam amid a small flock of milling sheep. The rough wooden corner post for the fence was gray with age and sturdy enough to last into the next century. With the Rocky Mountains behind him, Adam looked rugged enough to last longer.

Jillian carefully arranged her thoughts, just as she would in designing a layered collage—the most important image was on the top layer. Her personal "top" consisted of Adam and the problems between them. And that too soft kiss last night. It spoke of affection and concern, of gentleness and other odd notions she couldn't imagine Adam might feel for her. It tugged her from the safety of her dislike for him and took her into a realm too vulnerable for her liking. On impulse, she pulled to the side of the dirt farm road and parked her SUV. It was time to set the rules straight between Adam and herself.

Adam watched her as she tramped across the muddy field toward him. The thick pea-green army coat he wore had seen better days and his battered boots were locked to the mud. He looked as though he'd come thousands of miles to stand in this muddy field, the woolly sheep milling around him. The March wind picked at his shaggy hair and the sun gleamed upon it, blue-black, a contrast to the snow-capped, rugged mountains behind him. He wore the mix of Native American and Scots blood with that of a hunter, features harsh and unrelenting, his eyes steady upon her. He hadn't shaved, his jaw darkened with stubble that gave him a hard look, and the dark shadows beneath his steel-colored eyes said he hadn't slept any better than she.

"It was the kiss," he said quietly when she stood in front of him. "You've gnawed on it, and now you've come to tell me off again. I gave it as a gift, nothing more." That cool gray gaze took in her yellow sweater and jeans, the cold mud clinging to her white canvas shoes. In her excitement, she'd forgotten her coat and shivered from the cold wind; she wrapped her arms around herself, determined to lay out the rules for him. He would know, of course, that she was cold, her feet damp, and that her need to see him was impulsive. He would know that she was trained to hide her emotions, that coming to see him now was a need too fierce for her to control.

Her self-control and Adam weren't a stable mix.

She shook her head and her hand found the woolly pelt of a passing sheep, locking to it as an anchor. She braced herself to lie; she wouldn't give Adam the satisfaction of knowing he had disturbed her more with his tenderness than his anger. "I didn't have a second thought about that kiss. Not one."

He nodded solemnly, watching her rummage for words. His hand found a place near hers on the ewe. "It's good wool. Elspeth uses it in her work. The shearing ought to yield enough to keep her busy for a while."

She realized that Adam had moved slightly, sheltering her from the wind. "I know. It's beautiful to spin and to weave. The sheep are more of a tribute to her Scots ancestor, Una. In the summer they graze on Tallchief Mountain where heather has been planted to keep them company. When I work with Elspeth, spinning the wool, I can almost feel the peace of other women, doing the same, wrapping around me. The lanolin in the wool makes your fingers smooth, just as life should be. And to spin or weave a good solid product that will endure is wonderful. It's a lovely thing to know you can create a gift for someone you love, to keep them warm and comfortable. It's taken me a long time to find peace, Adam, and you're not destroying it."

"You're artistic, Jillian. I saw your work, but more than that. At Elspeth's you stroked the weave of her place mats, enjoying the texture and color. You nuzzled the children's hair, taking in their scents. You like candlelight and rich shadows, and you see beauty in a plain white coffee cup. Why did you let your parents' cold hearts force you into business?"

She didn't answer, lifting her face to the sun and closing her eyes. *I was the "good daughter." I wanted to be loved.* A girl who wants just a shred of love will do what she can to capture it. In another time, she'd tried so hard to please everyone and in the end, lost herself and her dreams. But they hadn't loved her any more for it—it was always Tom, the brother who would carry on the Green name.

She was raised to do just what she did—to understand business and to be the perfect wife of a man with political opportunities. Eventually, she admitted her marriage was a failure and that business wasn't the call of her heart. She'd gotten the degree and, after her marriage, had plodded to work every day, a stressed executive dressed in a suit, never fully leaving work at the office. Her life ran gray then, streaked with fear of the night and her marital bed. But she wouldn't give Adam the satisfaction of knowing that and the emptiness failure could bring.

"I'll be helping with the shearing and herding them out of the valley and up into the meadows on Tallchief Mountain. I'll enjoy camping there with them for a while. I love watching the lambs. Here, you're cold—"

With that, he took off his coat and slid it over her shoulders. "Put your arms in, Jillian. The better fit will keep the cold from seeping in."

Jillian shook her head, remembering when Adam had placed his high school athletic jacket over her shoulders in the same way. She didn't want the slightest comfort from him, a man who as a boy had torn her life apart. She would keep her composure. What he did, he could undo. The coat carried scents of sea salt and storms that could sweep her away. "Take it off."

He crossed his arms, the faded red sweatshirt he wore frayed at the collar and cuffs. "Your feet are freezing, and yet you're determined to hold your ground. Why?"

The coat smelled of man, wood smoke, animal and Adam. When she started to remove it, just as she wanted to remove him from her life, Adam picked her up. Her canvas shoes, sunken in the mud, stayed there. Before she could protest being carried by Adam, he placed her on top of the sturdy fence post. "Okay, spit it out. You have something to say, don't you?"

Adam was very strong, strong enough to control her easily. Another man had, forcing her. Yet Adam held her as he would a child, firmly, gently, yet not too close, his hands light upon her. The fear that had immediately swamped and paralyzed her slithered slowly away. "I don't like being handled."

"I didn't mishandle you. My hands were quite properly placed. Those are poor, pitiful shoes to be wearing when hunting a man, Jillian," he mocked gently.

"I wasn't hunting you. I just wanted to have a private conversation—" She stared at Adam, who had begun chafing her sock-covered feet. He tucked her feet beneath his arms and then folded them, tilting his head slightly as he listened. Jillian considered her predicament—and decided to deliver her message without losing as much dignity as possible. "Something has come up, a really good paying contract with good opportunities to draw attention to my work. I don't have time to relocate my equipment or my home just yet. Before I can do good work, I have to feel settled in my environment. I've found that harmony is very important to me. It will take all my energy and focus to do a good job on this new contract. I'm not established well just yet, and this will mean bigger clients. You're *not* going to ruin my chances, Adam."

"I wouldn't think of it," he murmured. "Not for a moment. But you could do with a good pair of boots if you're going to be coming after me."

It was difficult to retain her composure while sitting on top of a fence post, her feet warming under Adam's arms. She decided to venture a nothing-tried-nothing-gained. "Would you leave now, before the Tallchiefs sense that we don't like each other? To be honest, it's deeper, more fierce than that."

"Aye, it is." He nodded solemnly, his gray eyes considering her, shielded by those thick, black, glossy lashes. "It's cozy here in Amen Flats, Jilly-dear, with all my relatives around. I'd be a fool to leave a warm house and good food. I can pick up odd jobs here and there, enough for change money. Maybe you've got something I can do."

She stared at him and realized her mouth was open. "You're just tormenting me. You know full well that you are moving on when it suits you. I just tried to give you a sizable check to get you out of here. Why would I want to hire you? And what could you do for me?"

She didn't trust the searing heat in his eyes, quickly veiled by a mild smile and a shrug. "I'm a pretty good cook. I can do laundry and clean while you work. I can run errands for you. It's only the last of March now and someone has to carry in wood for the stove. April can still be chilly."

Adam Tallchief was asking her for a job. Jillian gripped the ancient wood of the fence post to keep from toppling from it. "Adam, that won't work. Not with us, and you know it. And I'm used to caring for myself. If I'm busy, the laundry can wait, so can the dishes."

Adam Tallchief, doing her laundry, making her bed, washing her dishes—in her house.... He'd take over the quiet life she'd build, her concentration destroyed. Her emotions concerning him were too fierce and unpredictable. She couldn't have him anywhere near her!

He wasn't deterred, watching her with those narrowed, steely eyes. Was he planning revenge?

"Maybe it's time for a change," he said quietly as the sheep moved around him. The wind snagged his hair, sailing it away from those rugged features. The impact of that hard, determined face took her breath away as he continued. "Maybe you'll become so busy you'll need help. I thought that since you're set on me not embarrassing my relatives, you might see what my talents are and help me get a good start for a meaningful life. In your times when you're not focusing and creating, of course, when you have to step away from work to refresh the well.''

"No," she returned firmly. Jillian tugged her now-warmed feet from his keeping. Somehow Adam understood that too much concentration led to dry, gritty eyes and slowed the creative process. In her first attempts at finishing contracts in lightning-quick time, she'd discovered it was much better to take refreshing breaks than to run herself dry. "I can't see any creative conversation happening between us.''

She couldn't have predicted that gentle kiss, either. She didn't like uncertainty and Adam managed to hand it to her at every turn.

"Well, then. I guess our business is finished, for now," Adam said. "It's a long way to the ground, Jillian. I can help you, or you can stay perched up there all day until someone notices you. Or you can be a nice, sensible girl, and let me carry you across the field and tuck you in your car.''

He glanced at a big ram watching them. "That old boy over there isn't a pleasant sort. We're not the best of friends yet, but I intend to get to him. For now he's leaving me alone, but you're a different matter. It's only a short distance, Jillian. You'll be safe with me.''

While Jillian hovered between safety and pride, Adam reached up his arms to her. It was for her to decide to trust him or not. Once she hadn't hesitated, leaping from the football field bleachers into his arms, trusting him. "Are you certain that ram is dangerous?''

"I've got a bruise on my backside that says he is.''

She studied the tilt of his head and the angle of that hard jaw. Her bargaining position wasn't good. "You'd really leave me here, wouldn't you?''

He shrugged and the wind caught his hair and his arrogance. In Jillian's mind, she could imagine his ancestor, Tallchief, standing just like that while he forced his captive bride to do as he bid. According to Tallchief legends, Una

hadn't liked the taming a bit and did a little of her own.
But then, Tallchief had stayed in one place with the brood
he and Una raised. He'd loved her as deeply as she loved
him and both fought for their marriage and home. In those
times, their marriage must have had many trials. He made
cradles to provide for them, and Una had sold her dowry.

But Adam wasn't likely to settle in one place for long—
"Fine," Jillian said dully.

He chuckled at that. "Ask me nicely, Jilly-dear."

She sighed heavily. Not really asking the question, she
plodded through the words as if doomed. "Will...you...
please...help...me."

"Adam," he insisted softly.

She sighed again and repeated, "'Adam.'"

She wasn't certain what she saw in his eyes, just that
steely spark, the look of a hunter hitting his mark. "Am I
going to owe you for this?"

"I'm certain the fee won't be too high for a successful
businesswoman such as yourself."

She had a degree in business, but it wasn't in her heart.
She preferred textures and colors and images. "I'm a free-
lancer now, Adam."

"Could that be because you don't want to be tethered to
anyone? Maybe we're alike in that. Maybe there is fear in
us, the fear of loving. It can be a dangerous thing, if mishandled."

She didn't want to discuss anything with him; his
thoughts were too deep, probing at hers. "I wouldn't call
drifting all over the world a freelance occupation."

She resented reaching out to him, bracing her hands on
his shoulders as he lifted her into his arms. "Maybe I've
had my fill of drifting. Maybe not. I've learned to take life
as it comes, to flow with it. Put your arm around my shoulder, Jillian," he ordered gently. "Even through the coat,
your shoulder is sharp against my chest."

Jillian closed her eyes, inhaled, and forced her arm to
lift and circle his shoulders. He was so big, too masculine,

and uncertainty speared her once more. Adam hadn't moved as he watched her. Their eyes met and Jillian looked away, afraid that he would see too much.

Adam walked slowly, carefully, across the field. Wrapped in his arms, wearing his coat and surrounded by his scents, it wasn't a journey she would forget soon. She could feel his warmth and strength. When she glanced at him, Adam's expression was grim, and on impulse she reached to push her fingers through his wind-blown hair, tethering it from his face.

His warm scalp, the crisp feel of his shaggy hair between her fingers shocked her. She hadn't expected to want to smooth it, to lock her fingers in it. She slid her hand away, returning it to his shoulder. "So that you can see better. It wouldn't do for you to misstep and we'd both go down in the mud. You could use a haircut."

He hesitated in his stride, but didn't look at her. "I could use a kiss."

"That's the price, is it? There always is. But we're not teenagers any longer, Adam—don't even think about a higher price."

Adam's scowl seared her, as though anger had leaped within him. Then he pushed it into a milder expression. "Sex, you mean? You and I? I'd have to think about that, but if it's not freely given, with caring and the heart involved, then it means little. One small friendly kiss I might take for a trade, but not a woman's body."

The past caught and lingered in the bright morning sunlight. At their first meeting, Adam had accused her of marrying Kevin for his family's money. The nagging questions leaped at her again. *Had she given herself to her husband and her marriage? Or had she been traded? Kevin had taken her as his right and had promptly fallen asleep—*

"I'm certain you've had plenty of kisses, and women, in your life." She wished she hadn't lobbed the words at him, trying to nudge information from him. Why should she care how many women Adam had known, or loved?

"I've had kisses, and a woman—one I thought I'd marry.
We were friends more than anything. Along the way, she
fell in love with someone else, and I had to wonder then
if we had ever loved. The pain should have been deeper,
but it wasn't."

"How do you know that?" She'd felt only relief when
Kevin had forsaken their marriage bed. It wouldn't do for
divorce papers to state that his wife was frigid—in Kevin's
mind, that would reflect upon his skill as a lover and damage the macho picture he sought as a young politician.

"I'd had something to compare it with. A girl, a long
time ago. She broke my heart. I wonder, at times, if it ever
mended enough to let another woman into it." He nodded
and continued to the barbed-wire fence. He placed her on
the other side and watched her remove his coat. He didn't
answer her goodbye as she handed it to him. She headed
in the direction of the Petrovnas', and looked in the rear-
view mirror. Adam stood, legs braced wide, holding the
coat and looking as if he'd wait forever.

Jillian rubbed her chest lightly and knew that the ache
in her heart was caused by memories that Adam had evoked
of a time when they were teenagers. She also noted that he
hadn't pressed his request for a kiss, that the decision had
been left to her.

She smoothed her fingertips over the steering wheel and
remembered how his hair had felt, crisp and straight,
gleaming in the sunlight. A shorter cut, a neat trim wouldn't
suit him, she decided. The shaggy, thick style matched his
untamed disposition; he traveled as he wished, and spoke
without sparing her. But then, he considered her family to
have caused his aunt's untimely death, didn't he? It was
only logical that he would pose questions to her that might
nag and hurt.

She'd wanted to marry Kevin. She'd wanted the dreams
that her friends were snatching at the time. She understood
him, his motives, how he needed to please his family. It
was a desperate need, matching her own. She liked and

respected him, and since she'd been raised in a family without love, she hadn't expected that favor. *Had she really sold herself for her family? When Kevin proposed, was she in love with love and not the man? Or did she want to get away from her parents and he was only the opportunity?*

Jillian pushed away the ugly thought. She had a great career opportunity and she was on her way to tell her friend.

Adam had nothing to do with her unrest, the questions that kept circling her. *"Sex, you mean?"* he'd asked. *"If it's not freely given, with caring and the heart involved, then it means little. One small friendly kiss I might take for trade, but not a woman's body.... A girl, a long time ago. She broke my heart. I wonder, at times, if it ever mended enough to let another woman into it."*

Who was that woman? What woman could hold Adam's heart?

The woodstove took the chill off his cabin that night, yet after a hard day's work repairing fence with Duncan Tallchief, Adam could not rest.

Jillian had cursed his coat and his life, Adam brooded darkly as he brought the coat to his face for the fiftieth time since she had worn it. He picked through the scents to the delicate one that was hers, like a rosebud just waiting to bloom. The scent had curled around him when he was a boy and her amber eyes had filled with him as he had carried her. He could have carried her forever with those eyes looking up at him, wary with a feminine curiosity. Why should he feel such tenderness for her? Why did she feel so precious in his arms?

Why should he want her still? Why did he hang on every word about her? Where was his pride? His anger and his revenge?

He looked at the small, white canvas shoes he'd soaked and cleaned as well as he could. They'd have to be returned in good time, but first he had work to do. Adam flipped open his laptop, prepared the electronic mail that sketched his ideas for Jillian, and signed the message "Sam."

He was known as "Sam" to boys and girls throughout the world who wrote to him. They had been his family until now, children happy with the toys and stories he created. Now he had Liam, Michelle, J.T. and the rest of the Tallchiefs.

He sat back in the chair, collected one of Jillian's shoes in his hand and waited as the electronic mail sailed over the telephone lines. Her reply was immediate. "Hi, Sam," it read. "Thank you for this wonderful opportunity."

She continued, assuring him that she'd love to meet him and was excited over the toys that she knew delighted children—and some adults, she'd added, causing Adam to smile. She understood his concepts perfectly and he would have rough ideas from her soon.

Adam tapped a return message. "I hope we can get better acquainted through our messages. I'd like to know you better. Sam the Truck is really a very close family with long-term relationships. Please send all ideas to Steve. Our marketing and sales department will consider them with me."

He tapped her shoe against his palm. Jillian didn't want any doors opened between Adam and herself, but perhaps she might respond to Sam. Deceptive? Yes. Was he unable to resist? Yes.

Adam located the electronic image Steve had sent him of Jillian's cabbage rose ad; she had submitted it as a sample of her work quality. Adam traced the layers of the screen roses and shook his head. *What was he doing? Asking for more pain?* She didn't believe him about her brother's crimes or her family's persuasion of the town to turn against Sarah and himself.

On his feet now, Adam remembered how her light touch on his hair had caused his heart to leap and his senses want to take. Wrapped in his thoughts, he placed his fingers on the prototype of the new Nancy the Flatbed Hauler, rolling the model toy gently back and forth on the table.

Jillian's fear of men was obvious, and trust wasn't a commodity they shared for each other. What was he doing? he wondered furiously as he decided to go make friends with the ram. It was safer than thinking about what tangled in the sunlight air earlier between Jillian and himself.

March slid into April, and with the Sam the Truck first contract dollars tucked into her bank account, Jillian finished Silver's ad. Half frightened that she would fail, she hurried to create new ones for Sam's approval; Nancy the Flatbed Hauler was set to launch in November, hitting the Christmas buyers just right.

Jillian listened to the early morning birds chirp and wished she could sleep. She tossed in the old bed, comforted by the creaks beneath her. The company had sent her all the previous marketing campaigns with models of the toys. Ideas for the designs kept plaguing her—and then Adam would stroll through them, tall, dark and not at all civilized.

Whatever had made her shove her hands through his hair like that? What was that wild impulse to match him on the most primitive level?

He hadn't left Amen Flats; in fact, he seemed to be settling in. A visitor at J.T.'s preschool, Adam told impressive stories of the world. According to grocery-store rumor, he made a fine bartender at Maddy's Hot Spot; he could toss glasses behind his back and catch them in the other hand which already held a bottle ready for pouring. One Ladies Only Night, he'd joined Patty Jo Black, a farm wife, in a sexy duet. There had been more than one feminine heart palpitating as he'd sung an Irish love song.

He wasn't taking up female invitations, though, and the women wondered how such a virile-looking, charming man could hold his sexual drive in control. Stories flew over the rooftops and through the beauty parlors and zoomed down the grocery store aisles. He was a catch, they said, a good-looking, single Tallchief male on the loose. They wondered what cruel witch had taken his heart and scarred it.

Jillian had never been in a country tavern, and she certainly wasn't trying Ladies Only Night while Adam was helping the bartender there. She'd heard that lemonade was served and the painting of the nude woman was draped in a sheet during the special night. No stories of intelligent children or husbands were told that night, and demerits were given for those who broke those rules.

She worked until her mind and her eyes were dry, trying to forget how carefully Adam had carried her that day.

She should have given him that kiss, just to prove that he meant nothing to her.

If he meant nothing to her, why did he stalk her restless dreams? She dreamed of the boy's face, replaced it with the man's furious one as he had been that first day. Then she replaced it once more with an expression she didn't understand.

Her parents had told her that Adam had lied. She couldn't defend him, not with her brother dead because of him. "Because of Adam...because of that boy..." The intense bitter litany had continued as her parents' drinking worsened.

They'd died after her marriage, and maybe, just maybe, one of the reasons she'd married was to escape them....

Lying in bed, she watched morning filter through the curtains and thought of Sam, how nice he was; how he seemed lonely and sensitive.

The slam of a vehicle door close to the house brought her upright. She pushed away the curtain to see Adam lifting a ladder from the back of his borrowed pickup truck. Jillian blinked as he carried it to her house.

She lost sight of him, leaped out of bed and walked to the door, tearing it open. Careless of the men's flannel pajamas she wore, Jillian held out her hand in a halt gesture. "You're up rather early in the morning for a bartender, aren't you? Stop right there."

Adam, dressed in a sweatshirt and bib overalls, ignored her and walked back to the pickup, unloaded paint cans and carried them to the house. "'Morning, Jillian. Did I wake you up?''

She rubbed her eyes and tried to leap from dozing in the quiet serenity of her home, feeling that her life was cruising the happy lane...to Adam Tallchief. "Why are you here?''

He walked up the porch steps and considered her as he removed a white canvas shoe from each of his pockets and handed them to her. "Liam and Michelle are busy with their new house plans. This place needs some fix-up.''

The shoes reminded her of how gently he'd carried her, as if he could carry her forever, and how safe she'd felt in his arms. *She'd almost snuggled down in that safe—almost. But she wasn't a snuggler and Adam wasn't safe.*

Jillian tossed the shoes to a chair, just as she hoped to discard that haunting moment. "Thanks. Adam, you need a regular job with benefits. Surely the house doesn't need painting *now*.''

"I've got a free day and the yard needs work, too.''

She tried for patience and failed. "I can do it, Adam. I just haven't had much time to spend on—''

He bent to gently kiss her lips, stunning her once more. "You're working too hard, Jillian. You've got shadows under your eyes and you're pale. Tell that slave driver to back off and give you time to rest.''

"Sam is a very nice man. I'm thrilled to be working for him.''

Adam snorted, dismissing her opinion. "You think highly of a man you don't know.''

Jillian pushed her mussed hair back from her face and locked herself into defending Sam. "I know him. We're communicating all the time. And not about business, either. He's become a good friend.''

"Uh-huh. That technique makes employees work better.''

"Just what would you know about that?'' she fired at

him, and wished she hadn't. Adam had a way that caused
her to respond recklessly. She much preferred the control
that had served her for a lifetime.

He smiled at that, a boyish grin she hadn't expected.
"Are you always a grump in the morning, Jilly-dear? Or
are you just overjoyed to see me? By the way, you look
warm and cuddly and rosy, quite the inviting picture."

At the sound of a small dog yapping, Jillian leaned to
one side of Adam's broad shoulders. She found Mrs. Haw-
kins on her early morning jog, peering at her visitor. She
would have seen Jillian in her pajamas, just bidding Adam
goodbye with a kiss—the image wasn't good, it spoke of
an all-night visit and a good-morning-see-you-later-honey.

"Adam, get in here," Jillian ordered as she grabbed the
front of his sweatshirt. His eyes narrowed and he didn't
move for a heartbeat, as if choosing to stand or to obey.
Then he allowed her to tug him inside, shutting the door
behind him. She rubbed her forehead, trying to sort out a
late night, a too early morning and Adam's sultry, dark look
as it roamed down her body.

The hunger was there, veiled by black lashes and riding
that firm mouth. Instead of the fear she'd expected, the need
to— Jillian turned away from him, shaking with the thought
that she was too susceptible to Adam, her defenses down
in the morning and her sexual urges—if she had them—on
the rise. The hunger in her body was nonsense, of course.
She had accepted long ago that she was a frigid woman,
terrified of men. She crossed her arms, digging her fingers
into her flesh; she wanted to fling herself upon him and kiss
and take and see—

With a rough sound, Adam spun her around. His stormy
hot look equaled the emotions inside her as Jillian shivered
and ached and scowled up at him.

"Afraid?" he asked too softly, the deep sound seeming
to wrap around her, tugging at her sensually.

She lifted her chin, glaring at him. "Not a bit."

His fingers caught her hair, firmly but gently, holding

her as he leaned close to study her. "Just do it. Then we'll both know."

Her hands were on his chest now, the heavy beat racing beneath her touch. She tried for calm and failed. Then passion sprang from her keeping and she reached upward even as his arms circled her waist, tugging her to him.

His mouth fused to hers, and this time the gentleness wasn't there, only the hunger and the heat seeking hers.

Jillian's senses filled with him, tossed away her fear and gave as he sought, feeding her own needs. His breath warmed her face, the soap and clean air scents blending with that of Adam. *Adam.*

The woman in her knew his body shook from desire, and welcomed the thought that she had called it forth. She understood that hardening of his body, but not the melting of her own, that soft, dewy ache, low and intimate. His hand found her bottom, caressed it, pressing her closer. She realized that her hips had flowed against him, a natural, sexual rhythm. His breathing had changed, rough now, uneven, and her fear came slipping back until it devoured her.

She pushed away and Adam looked down to where her pajama top had come unbuttoned, the space between her breasts pale in the shadows. His fingertip strolled down that space before she gathered the edges together with shaking hands. "So we know now, don't we?" he asked huskily.

And she knew that he would want more, and so would she. The calling was too primitive, her first taste. Her heart still beat hard and fast within her chest, her breasts had peaked, nudging the flannel material in her response to him.

Then as though nothing had happened between them, Adam moved to her computer, which had been left on all night. He scanned the design she planned for Nancy, and picked up the as yet unmarketed toy, studying it. "Nice."

How could he dismiss her, just like that? Just after he'd held her tight against him and uttered those lovely, deep, hungry sounds— Jillian shook her head. Only Adam had the ability to tear her temper from its cool hiding place.

She sat and tried to regain her calm, and found sturdy anger instead. "In contrast to you, the man commissioning that work is understanding and sweet."

Adam held very still, a big man taking too much space in a small, feminine setting. "Have you met him?"

"No. But he's a very gentle man. He sends me e-mail. He's very thoughtful and creative. I adore him. That mixed bouquet of flowers is from him, a very nice welcoming present to his 'Sam family.' I'm hoping to meet him. I think we could be very good friends. He's generous, too. Once he found that J.T. was in preschool, he sent Sam the Truck toys to his class. I think he's lonely, and I like him. He's very, very sensitive and has a good sense of humor, too," she repeated, realizing that she sounded defensive.

"I see. I'd better get to work then," Adam said, tossing Nancy back to the desk. "That color is a bit off, isn't it? The toy has a deeper shade of rose and the eyes need more feeling. Put a speck or two just there and there, and the eyelashes on the model are more distinct. That piece of information is too low for impact," he offered, pointing to the screen.

"You think so?" she asked, waylaid by Adam's input to her design. She came to stand beside him, studying her work. She leaned close, concentrating on the design. "I suppose I could try. It's easily undone. I've only just started on this, you know. I've had to read his storybooks to get the feel he wanted, family and warmth, of caring and trying to do the best you can. Sam is about values and love and friendship."

"Well, I'm not an artist, so my opinion isn't worth much." He glanced down to where her breast had brushed his arm, and his gaze met hers, the hunger in it taking away her breath. "Aye, I'd say so. I'd better get to work," he said unevenly.

"So should I." She wondered why she couldn't move, why Adam's gaze held her there as if the past and the future tangled between them, each unable to let go.

Then he smoothed her hair and his eyes followed the motion, his expression a mixture of tenderness and regret. He tugged a strand and asked, "Would you have had me do anything less, Jillian? I had my pride and obligations. We all have choices and now you have yours."

Her bare feet locked to the floor and she couldn't move, wondering at the flaming kiss they'd shared as it throbbed through her veins, still heating her. She wrapped her arms around her shivering body and rocked slightly. She tried to push away that kiss, the kiss of a man and a woman that had nothing to do with the past or revenge.

Yet it lingered and taunted and hungered as Adam looked down at her. The pulse in his throat beat heavily, those steel-gray eyes tracing her blush and brushing her lips. He tensed and leaned toward her, and then with a rough sound he opened the door. "I think the painting can wait."

"So do I. Please leave." She was afraid of herself now, because with Adam, she lacked that classy, cool control, her protection.

Why did her heart leap at the sight of him? Why had she kissed him? And without reserve, for it was no cool peck they'd shared, but a stormy tempest that smacked of passion and more—and she'd wanted him in her bed, staked out beneath her....

Five

At noon on a mid-April day, Tallchief Mountain soared above the valley in a mix of elegant pines and fir, meadows and rough, jutting rocks. A late, light snowfall gleamed on the meadows that would be lush with summer grass.

Adam lifted his face to the icy wind that sailed around the rugged cliffs and over the pines. He could still smell Jillian's feminine scent and still taste her hunger on his lips from that morning two weeks ago. For just that moment, soft and warm in his arms, she'd given him an insight more dangerous than her anger. Her bottom had been curved and firm in the palm of his hand. She'd stood on tiptoe and leaned against him, the shape of her breasts too near not to hold—but he hadn't, at least he'd had that much control.

Fever for her had hardened his body, and now he brooded on a cold mountain about the past and a riveting need that left him with an uncomfortable ache. Climbing the rough trail didn't free him of the hunger and he'd known that painting the house with her in it was asking for trouble. *He'd thought he could resist her, and after just that one hungry taste, he knew that being near Jillian would cause his body to hum and his heart to race. That soft, sweet, simmering look she sent him had almost... Little had kept him from carrying her to her bed.*

After years of guarding his relationships, Adam had to admit that she'd torn away his protective layers; he'd wanted to make love to her, to seal or to end a need that had threaded through his life, destroying him for other women.

Adam shook his head and thought how foolish he was, unable to wipe the taste of her away, and in desperation, tramping up a muddy, overgrown mountain trail. He was forty years old, and just as desperate—maybe more so— for Jillian as he had been at eighteen.

"That does little for my confidence," he said to himself as he slung the Tallchief plaid over his shoulder and settled down to brood upon a big black rock spotted with age and worn by rain. At various times in his life, he'd felt just as old and worn, especially during Sarah's last illness.

He certainly didn't feel as if he were old when Jillian was near. All body and heart parts accelerated immediately. He propped a boot upon a fallen log and thought of how narrow and delicate Jillian's feet had felt in his hands.

It was better than thinking of how she felt in his arms, warm from bed and drowsy from sleep, and clad in oversize men's pajamas that made her look even more feminine.

She thought little of him, but seemed to adore Sam.

It was a stupid thing to do, trying to hold on to her before life and their past erupted, separating them forever.

Just down there in Amen Flats, she was working on a new Sam ad campaign. Adam smiled briefly. Jillian was good and would be building a clientele. She suited the community better than he.

Adam lifted his face to the wind again, waiting for the call of new places to beckon him. Yet none came.

Nothing came to him in the wind and the cold but the

need to hold Jillian close and to feel her heart beat against his.

Adam rubbed his jaw and settled his fingers to stroke the wool around his shoulders. Jillian had said she experienced pleasure in spinning and weaving, the timeless craft women shared. Her home had the look of a loving woman making her nest, tending the serenity of it.

"I work from my home," she had written Sam. "It's comfortable and small and warm in the worst storms we have here in Wyoming. I don't have children, but if I did, I would certainly read them your stories. I've just seen a whole family of men and women down on the floor, playing with your toys. It was heartwarming."

"Let me make this clear," Adam had written as Sam. He had written the same to other contractors and employees, but with Jillian the message was more personal. "If you are in need of anything to make you more comfortable, please don't hesitate to ask. We are a family here at Sam the Truck. If you would like an office in which to do your work, that can be provided. If you would like to relocate closer to our factory, that's possible. We want you to be happy. I want you to feel that you can write me at any time and discuss anything at all."

"Thank you so much," she had returned. "But I love this little country community and there is a family here that I adore. There is also a big reason why I cannot leave, but I am capable of handling the problem."

"Think of us as your family," he had written amid other information about Sam the Truck company benefits. "Is there anything I can do to help?"

Jillian had replied with a few questions and written, "No. I've just met someone who I knew a long time ago. He's upset me, but I can deal with him."

Sam would not have written the reply to that—but Adam's curiosity had driven him on, even as he damned himself. "A romantic interest? I've only had one experience, but I know how it can tear at the heart. If you need someone to talk with, I'm here."

"Thank you so much. But this man only reminds me of other times, nothing more. He'll be on his way soon. He's a drifter and brooding, and always out of work. I don't know that he does work, really, just odd jobs. I pity his poor relatives who are basically supporting him. I'll like being a part of the Sam family. I have lost my own and am so lonely at times. Families are what everyone should have. I've seen wonderful love and care here in Amen Flats, more than in my own family. I love being with them, but after this problem is settled and my work completed, I will be moving. This will not interfere with our relationship."

Her "problem" meant one Adam Tallchief…a drifter… always out of work…his poor relatives who are basically supporting him. Adam hiked his jacket collar up against the wind's cold nip and lowered his face slightly into the warm Tallchief plaid that Elspeth had woven for him. He kept little with him, traveling light, but the plaid seemed a part of him now.

Jillian might never discover that he was Sam. In her messages, she was not only professional, but still soft and sweet. And she loved the Tallchief family.

What did he know about families? He'd only had Sarah—Sarah, who he couldn't protect at eighteen and who still touched his life, even in the wind hurling around the trees and the rocks of Tallchief Mountain. He held her close inside him, keeping his grief from others.

Maybe Jillian was right—that J.T. would miss Adam when he left. Liam had changed his life to give his son a heritage. Yet he posed a nagging question to Adam—why Sarah hadn't known their parents' destination, or the reason for it—other than a short vacation.

Sarah had always portrayed his parents as loving. Why then would a mother and father leave a three-year-old boy recovering from a cold, without a contact number?

Adam wondered if more information rested in Aunt
Sarah's safe-deposit box in Iota. Whatever remained of
their parents, he and Liam should know.

The kinship that should have been between them as children was there as men—some siblings did not have that,
and Adam wanted the best for his brother and family. Rocking a four-year-old boy while he dozed and playing trucks
with J.T. on the floor had been incredible—the warmth of
Liam and Michelle's home a treasure Adam would always
keep.

He'd traveled his entire adult life, living out of duffel
bags. There was history here, a family blending together,
loving each other. He wasn't a part of that, and yet blood
told him that he was. What could he give them, other than
a few toys, baby-sitting and help with fix-up jobs?

Adam leaned back on the rock. The birds filling the
bright blue sky used mountain drafts to soar without moving their wings. For whatever reason, Sarah had wanted
Jillian to give him those feathers. Whatever was brewing
between Jillian and himself wasn't calm; he'd gotten a taste
of how the unexpected need for her could erupt and devour
him.

Jillian hadn't had a family, not like the Tallchiefs. Maybe
she deserved a taste of warmth and love.

Adam inhaled sharply; she certainly could have used the
protection years ago. And Sarah, too, a woman raising a
son alone, troubled by poor health and turmoil. *Sarah*....

He noted the cutting journey of a hawk across the sky.
Liam deserved to know about Sarah, her strength and unwavering love. Perhaps now was time to open his aunt's
safe-deposit box. Her things should be divided with Liam.
Whatever rested in that box was also his to know and share.

"So that's why." Liam tossed Sarah's letter onto the
dining room table with the rest of her things, and those
precious to Jamie and Tina Tallchief. "In this letter, she
admits to calling Pauline Tallchief—the mother of Duncan

and the rest—to waylay her, to keep her from coming to claim you. There was no record of it in the letters that Elspeth has from our parents and from her mother, because Sarah didn't want written records.''

Liam's fury shook the room. ''Sarah's mother had a heart attack and passed away just after our parents left. By the time news of our parents' wreck arrived, *she knew* she wasn't letting you go. *She deliberately lied.* She said that your cold had turned worse, and you had just died of pneumonia. At the time, Pauline had no idea that you were alive. That's why she didn't try to contact you. She didn't double check that woman's lie.''

Liam's bitterness echoed in the room after he stopped talking, his eyes bright with anger. ''And you think she loved you. What kind of a woman would do a thing like that? Say a boy was dead in order to keep him for herself?''

''The kind of woman who had just lost her mother, her sister and a man she loved. A kind of woman who had no one else left in her life.''

''It wasn't right. She shouldn't have done it.''

Adam didn't answer; he knew how painful the letter would be to Liam because he'd experienced that same outrage and shock. But he didn't regret showing his brother the startling, condemning letter; Liam had a right to know the truth and to give it to his son.

The drive to Iota from Amen Flats took a solid day and a half, across a crooked mountain road. Years ago, his parents had planned ''a two-day hop,'' moving slower with an infant. Down a craggy mountain bank that ended in a rushing stream, they'd died; Liam had been salvaged from the car wreck by a childless couple and passed off as their own. The distance was only a few hundred miles, but it bridged thirty-six years. The round trip had taken Adam four days—he'd spent a day weighing whether to tell Liam about Sarah. Truth wasn't always easy, but Liam deserved nothing less.

Adam glanced at J.T. He was asleep on the carpet, amid

his Sam the Truck toys, and oblivious to the fact that the
adults in Liam's home were facing a stormy past more
fierce than the April night's raging outside.

In the safe-deposit box had rested the court order assign-
ing Sarah as four-year-old Adam's legal guardian. That decision had taken an entire year of wrangling.

Now, over the old brooches and papers and coins rested
the letter from Sarah to Adam. Words of love mixed with
harsh truths.

"I never married. Jamie had been my only love, but
he'd loved and married my sister. I was happy for
them, but knew I would never marry or have children,
and settled into my lonely fate.

"I'd looked forward to Liam's birth, because that
would give me more time with you. I'd had thoughts
of running away with you then, because they had another child. But I loved them, and baby Liam when
he came.

"I knew exactly what I was doing when I lied to
the investigators about your parents' death—and
Liam's. My mother had just passed away, and I
couldn't bear losing everyone in my life. I was afraid
that if I told them the truth of where they'd intended
to go, the investigators would discover the Tallchief
family. Matthew and Pauline already had a brood of
their own, but I knew they would want you. Tina had
told me so much about them. I knew they could give
you more than I could. But I wanted you for my own,
to love as my own son and to raise you without inter-
ference. I was afraid that the Tallchief family would
snare your love away from me. And selfishly, I wanted
to keep both the people that I loved close, a part of
each in you."

Adam picked up the letter that had waited for over
twenty-five years, when Sarah first began to fail badly. He
reread her admission.

"I wanted a new life, without danger that the Tall-chiefs would come after you, claiming you. I found a good-paying job with a tax firm in New Pony, and we started life as mother and son. How happy I was. I could not tell you this sooner, because I could not bear to feel your anger, or to lose your love. My friend has a chest in storage that rightfully belongs to you. She didn't know where we went, or what was in it, but I knew she'd keep it safe."

Michelle came to rest her hand on Liam's shoulder and his immediately sought hers. "We've lost a lifetime together," Liam said, his expression grim. "I've come to hate letters from the past. You never know what they'll open up."

"Shush, Liam," Michelle admonished softly. "It was a letter from your foster mother that brought you here. She loved you enough to hide the truth in a letter, in her Bible, and it waited for you.... Sarah loved you, Adam. If she'd have known Liam, she would have loved him, too. Try not to think too harshly of Sarah," Michelle murmured softly.

"At first, holding that letter for the first time, I did. And part of me is still angry. But she loved me, and I was her son, a part of her sister she couldn't bear parting with. It's a good thing to be wanted as a child. Some aren't. It will take some time to settle my feelings, but I can't hate her. She never faltered, never failed me, not once. I've come to know that there are few people like her in the world."

Liam's hard expression said there was little forgiveness in his heart. He'd lived a harsh life with the man who had stolen him from their parents' wrecked car. He met Adam's eyes, the same shade of brooding gray as his own. "Look at us. Grown men who have missed a lifetime together. Why didn't you open the box sooner, Adam?"

The words framed a terse demand rather than a light

question. But Adam understood Liam's emotions—they mirrored his own when he'd first opened the letter. "It didn't matter to me before coming here and meeting you, but I wanted you and your family to have your share. I also found Sarah's friend's daughter. She'd been keeping a trunk in storage, a promise to her mother, and it's in the back of the pickup. It's a big thing and heavy. I thought I'd let you adjust to Aunt Sarah's letter first."

"I may never adjust to it," Liam said broodingly. "Let's get the trunk."

When the trunk was in Liam's home, the contents neatly unpacked, it was a mix of the family's Native American, Scots, English and Inuit heritage across the surface of the family dining table, all stuffed around an old, obviously beloved wooden cradle. Scrimshawed walrus tusks mixed with leather poetry books, arrowheads, a hunting knife in a fringed sheath, a book on English gardens—and the rest had clearly been cherished. The heirlooms and mementos were meant to be passed from generation to generation, from husband to wife and back again. *Sarah hadn't wanted him to explore his heritage—or his potential relatives. Guilt must have made her keep the feathers, saving them for him. How that deception must have cost her... Oh, Sarah....*

"I'd like a few things of Sarah's saved back for me, if you would. I'd like to see them now and then, when I come back to see my nephews and the new baby. The rest is your share."

"'Share'? What do these things matter when we've lost so much?" Liam asked bitterly. "And I don't want anything to do with Sarah's things. I want no part of her."

Adam was still numb from the discovery, but anger mixed with love. "I loved Aunt Sarah. She may not have done the right thing, but she loved me. I was like her son. She's a part of me."

"You're leaving, aren't you, Adam?" Michelle asked

quietly. "You wanted us to have this before you left. You wanted everything for Liam and J.T. and the new baby."

Adam toyed with the oval locket that Sarah had always worn, the picture of her sister and of him. He loved her and nothing would change that. Trying to hold someone you loved close and dear wasn't a crime of the heart. Then there was Jillian and the knowledge that he wanted her desperately; that what ran between them was not mild enough to be pushed aside. "Perhaps it's best."

"Stand and fight," Liam challenged darkly. "You think you have no place here. Well, you do."

"Aye, you do," Michelle agreed softly. "With us, with Liam."

"You'll take care of Liam, that's clear enough. I see the love between you, and feel it, too."

"And who will take care of you, Adam?" Michelle persisted.

"I've managed my life until now," Adam said coolly, unused to family entering his life, the questions that were given because they cared. He didn't want them to worry about him.

"It's Jillian O'Malley, isn't it?" Liam said, eyeing Adam. "It's clear to see there's trouble between you. I heard she stepped out of her way to avoid you on Main Street. Another time, you bowed to her as she passed, turning up her nose. And to say nothing of the gossip raging around town about you leaving her house in the early morning, giving her a goodbye kiss while she was still dressed in her pajamas."

"The town snoop got her details mixed up a bit. I was coming to paint the house. I was doing *you* a favor. She rented it from you."

Liam settled back in his chair, studying his brother intently, sifting the facts and the look of a man brooding over a woman. "Try again. That house was just fixed up last year. The paint was good, so was the caulking. You wanted to see her.''

Adam had needed few people in his adult life, and the truth of Liam's statement nettled. "I can manage without Ms. O'Malley. And another coat wouldn't have hurt it."

He stood to pull on his coat and Liam stood, too, reaching for his. Clearly he wasn't going to let Adam walk out into the night feeling alone and hurt. He looked at Michelle, who said with an impish grin, "I know. There's only one real place for Tallchief males to conference about women—Maddy's Hot Spot. It's a tradition."

"I can manage my own problems," Adam stated firmly. "And Jillian O'Malley isn't one of them."

"Sure." Liam's broad grin said he didn't believe Adam. "Come on. What are brothers for, if not to talk about women." He winked at Michelle and added, "And how to handle them."

As an adult, Adam wasn't used to letting anyone into his life. Liam needed time to adjust to Sarah's misstep and the cost to the brothers. They were men now, Sarah was gone, and the gap might never be bridged. But Adam knew that Liam worried for him, and didn't want him brooding alone. They'd both have to give and take and understand, if they were to become closer. "I could use a brew with a brother, my only brother."

Adam's feelings after Jillian's kiss were not likely to be gentled. But at least he would keep his distance from her. It wasn't the traveler's wind beckoning to him this time, it was the knowledge that if he came near her, he'd want more than a kiss—whatever their past.

He studied how Michelle seemed to understand Liam's pain, his anger; even now, her eyes, as they met Adam's, were worried. She held her husband tight, protectively, the wife comforting the husband.

And Adam was an outsider, uneasy with the intimacy of love, of family. It would be easier for everyone if he went on his way.

* * *

Adam awoke early the next morning to a slice of blinding sunlight in his eyes and Jillian standing above him. She held the glass that had just been emptied of its freezing water—directly onto Adam's face. "So you're leaving, are you?"

He caught her wrist and struggled to find reality. "I thought you wanted me to."

"You're running, Adam Tallchief. You're running from family and ties, and people loving you. You don't think I can have *that* on my conscience, do you? That I chased you away from a family who wants you? From a brother you've never known? Let alone J.T.," she demanded. "You've stayed too long, you brought all those lovely things back for your brother, Michelle says Liam is worried you'll leave and the next time you'll see each other will be—"

He freed her wrist and sat up slowly. He shook his head, trying to clear it of sleep. In the early morning, his cabin should have been quiet, but the woman banging the metal coffeepot, filling it, was set upon destroying any peace he had. She glared over her shoulder at him, while Adam couldn't help admiring the fine curves of her backside in those tight jeans. "What's the matter, Adam?" she demanded. "Surely women have woken you up before?"

He shook his head and instantly regretted it—and the alcohol that had caused the pain. He'd rarely shared a night like the past, with a brother and a family of others, and the knowledge that Jillian Green O'Malley was likely the only woman for him. "I told you there was only one woman, one that I thought I'd marry. There hasn't been one since. And if this is how it is with a woman around—a wake-up call of icy water and an argument already on the griddle— then I'd just rather not."

Jillian wasn't backing off. The sunlight coming from the window caught the flame in her auburn hair and caressed the neat curves beneath her yellow sweater and blue jeans.

"You hunted down something that means very much to Liam, if not to yourself. You did that for him and his family. They love you even more now. You can't just take their hearts and leave. You've got to make something of yourself. I'm going to help you," she continued. "We'll find something you can do and we'll focus on that."

To tell her that as Sam, he'd worked for hours alone, designing the toys he loved, wouldn't do. Or that he sometimes liked jobs that allowed to mix with people—on his terms. Maddy's Hot Spot was rich with small-town lore and love, and he'd wound it around him. But then, he couldn't tell her the many hours devoted to Sam the Truck, could he? He cursed himself again for the idea of keeping Jillian close.

He studied her and rose to his feet, staring down at his body. He was only wearing his boxer shorts and considering Jillian's curved bottom, remembering the feel of it in his hand, had taken its hardening toll. He felt vulnerable, an unusual emotion in his adult life. "I do plenty. You can't just come into a man's home and start yammering at him, Jilly-dear."

He looked at the coffee brewing on the stove, the morning nectar that would make his life bearable, and loved her.

Adam blinked and shook his head. *He loved her. He'd loved her all this time.*

The thought was enough to make him brace a hand against the wall, needing it for strength. With a tremendous effort, he moved to the washbasin. He washed his face and brushed his teeth and the truth wasn't going anywhere. Dressed in a black sweatshirt and jeans, he went outside, and when he came back, not even the cold morning air had wiped away one fact—he loved Jillian.

There was nothing he could do, while she stood there with her hands on her hips, glaring at him, but to take her in his arms and kiss her. Apparently, surprise attacks fared him better, because her fear hadn't had time to move in before that lift of her lips met his, her body pressed against his.

The full, steamy tear of desire seared through him, as he barely kept his hands from caressing her breasts and her bottom—that delicious, soft, round curve. Later, he would congratulate himself on his good behavior when his body and mind were consumed with desire.

Jillian breathed deeply and with the flat of her hands upon his chest, pushed herself away. While his arms and heart ached to reach for her, his mind heard a distinct clang of a warning bell. To do something, anything, he went to the coffeepot that was now bubbling over, the droplets skittering, sizzling on the stove's black surface. He felt like that, his instinct to hold and to comfort her tearing at him. But there would be none of that—she was pale and shaking, those golden eyes wide and fearful upon him. "Well, now. What are we going to do about this? Do you want to tell me about it, Jillian? It was O'Malley, wasn't it? And now you're terrified of a man's touch."

Jillian locked her hands to the back of the chair. She wanted to run away from the total male power Adam exuded while holding her. Her heart thudded so hard, it chased every other sound away. Caught in the heat of what she wanted, driven by it, she had responded to Adam. Fiercely needing his taste, the fire building between them, she had coursed into fever—

The sound of the coffee hissing on the old black cook stove had slid through her senses and suddenly fear sprang alive and terrifying.

"O'Malley?" Adam pressed, as he filled the cup with hot water from the kettle and placed a tea bag in it. "Here, drink this. You look like you could use it."

He placed it on the table, while a distance away, he sipped his coffee. Jillian swam through a living nightmare, and focused on concealing it. But she'd been stripped bare before Adam; *he knew.*

"Sit down, Jillian," he ordered quietly.

She eased into the chair, her body shaking as she held the cup. The tiny ripples in the tea reflected the chilling terror she sought to control. She'd hidden it from others, but now, suddenly, with Adam, it had erupted.

"How's work going?" he asked as calmly as if nothing had happened.

She nodded, reliving the journey from hunger for him, that spreading warmth, to fear just sliding away. "Good."

"How's Sam?"

She nodded again, struggling to think clearly. She knew he was working to bring her back to reality, to an everyday common moment that was safe. "He's a wonderful man. So thoughtful. I've been on the project for a week, and he says it's good, really good with minor alterations. Oh, Adam, that project was for a national magazine ad, and next I get to design something for Nancy's packaging. A little brochure to go inside, Nancy's birth papers, the Truck Land Assembly Plant and the design on the packaging box."

Adam frowned at that. "He's probably getting more than he's paying for.... Did I scare you?"

"No," she answered slowly, as if adjusting from a happy lane to a darker one. "But it's hard to separate everything. I haven't been close to a man since my marriage. I went into counseling, and I thought I had put it behind me. Apparently I haven't. I think Kevin tried, but at the last moment, he lost control and I froze. I suppose all men do that—"

Adam's dark curse slammed into the room. "No, they don't. It might cause discomfort, but a man can stop."

"He didn't. We didn't have relations for the last four years of our five-year marriage, but Kevin didn't want a divorce so soon. His parents said it wouldn't look good for his political career. We came to a living arrangement that suited us both and a separation that was so cold and businesslike that it was almost as if we'd never known each other. I accepted the fact that sex wasn't likely to be on my life list. It's too primitive and I can't bear it.''

Adam sat slowly beside her. Her hand was cold in his easy, warm grasp. Not wanting to frighten her, he lifted it to his lips, kissing the center, then pressed it against his cheek.

She could feel the bones beneath skin roughed by stubble, the tips of her fingers resting in that thick straight hair. There was so much warmth there, just at her fingertips, intimate against her palm. It felt as if she could wrap her fist around it, as if something real were just within her grasp, an anchor that would moor her in the worst of storms. But then she'd given up those dreams long ago.

He took her other hand and cherished it just the same, until her hands framed his face. He looked at her, those gray eyes dark beneath the shield of his black lashes. ''You see? Nothing to be afraid of.''

Nothing except the fierce desire that still clung to her, battling with the past and her fear.

''How about going over to Elspeth's and seeing if we can have breakfast with her brood?'' he asked, smiling as he slid his fingers between hers, their hands meeting, soft palm to calloused one.

The intimacy of male and female intertwined brought other images to Jillian's mind, such as how he had looked down at her, that pure flash of desire hardening his features. She saw herself holding him against her, her lips still tasting him. Who was that other woman, the one who had escaped her fear, just for that moment?

The kiss he'd given her earlier had ignited this one, because she'd been brooding about it—and Adam. He'd hurt her family dearly, and yet— She should just…and yet—

Adam slid one hand free and reached to tap her forehead with it. ''Don't think so hard, Jillian. Spend some time with Elspeth—she's calming, and you could weave if it suits you. That's what you like to do, isn't it? Put the pieces together to make an image you like?''

They had been pretty little images, the life she'd expected with Kevin. But reality tore them apart.

"I'm not going to breakfast at Elspeth's with you. There's enough gossip about us already with you kissing me that morning you came to paint the house. And you didn't finish it. I can't be to blame because Liam and Michelle can't get a handyman to take care of the cottage. I'll paint it myself." She stopped, considering how she had never maintained a house. Only Adam could make her forget caution. "It will be good exercise. As for Elspeth, yes, that is a good idea. But I'll go by myself."

"Aye, you do that, Jilly-dear. But she's already invited me to breakfast. It's a family affair. Liam is to bring a trunk filled with family mementos, and Elspeth and Sybil are going to investigate it. They'll try to match it with Elizabeth's and Una's journals."

"Michelle told me of Sarah's letter, how it had devastated Liam. She said you had closed yourself away from Liam, loyal to Sarah, but angry, too. She doesn't believe you've ever truly allowed yourself to grieve for Sarah, that you hoard her close to you."

"My sister-in-law should take care of her own family and not worry about me."

"Don't you run away from this family, Adam. Now you're here and you'll have to deal with the consequences—" She frowned, noting the small cut on his thumb. It was in the exact same place as Liam's and Duncan's and all the rest of the Tallchief family; it symbolized that they had claimed him with the mixing of their blood. She touched the cut lightly. "You could turn your back on that? I don't think so."

"And what are you turning your back on, Jillian? And when was the last time you painted the exterior of a house?"

She knew how to host a party, how to invite guests and seat them to advantage. She knew proper crystal and good linen and smart menus. She knew business and computer

Play The Lucky Hearts Game

and get...
FREE BOOKS & a FREE GIFT...
YOURS to KEEP!

Yes! I have scratched off the silver card. Please send me my **2 FREE BOOKS** and **FREE GIFT**. I understand that I am under no obligation to purchase any books as explained on the back of this card.

Scratch Here!
then look below to see what your cards get you...

326 SDL DH4E
225 SDL DH4D

NAME   (PLEASE PRINT CLEARLY)

ADDRESS

APT.#   CITY

STATE / PROV.   ZIP/POSTAL CODE

Twenty-one gets you
2 FREE BOOKS and
a **FREE GIFT!**

Twenty gets you
2 FREE BOOKS!

Nineteen gets you
1 FREE BOOK!

TRY AGAIN!

Offer limited to one per household and not valid to current Silhouette Desire® subscribers. All orders subject to approval.

Visit us online at
www.eHarlequin.com

DETACH AND MAIL CARD TODAY!

(S-D-02/02)

© 1998 HARLEQUIN ENTERPRISES LTD. ® and TM are Trademarks owned by Harlequin Books S.A. used under license.

The Silhouette Reader Service™ — Here's how it works:
Accepting your 2 free books and gift places you under no obligation to buy anything. You may keep the books and gift and return the shipping statement marked "cancel." If you do not cancel, about a month later we'll send you 6 additional books and bill you just $3.34 each in the U.S., or $3.74 each in Canada, plus 25¢ shipping & handling per book and applicable taxes if any.* That's the complete price and — compared to cover prices of $3.99 each in the U.S. and $4.50 each in Canada — it's quite a bargain! You may cancel at any time, but if you choose to continue, every month we'll send you 6 more books, which you may either purchase at the discount price or return to us and cancel your subscription.

*Terms and prices subject to change without notice. Sales tax applicable in N.Y. Canadian residents will be charged applicable provincial taxes and GST.

graphics. But home upkeep hadn't been her experience, and Adam knew it; he knew where all her touch points were and he was pushing— She stood and lifted her chin. "I'm going."

He swept out a hand in a grand gesture toward the door. "Fare thee well. But next time you wake me up, try to be a little bit more considerate, will you? I'm sensitive."

She scoffed at that. "You've got to make something of yourself, Adam. You're forty years old and not a job with benefits in sight."

"I'm old enough to know what's best for me," he stated, locking his gaze with hers. "Oh, I love kissing you, Jillian—when you kiss me back."

She turned quickly, fearing he would see her blush. Then Adam's lips were warm against her neck, just here and just there, one side and then the other. She fought leaning back against him, from arching her throat to allow him more. "Come with me to breakfast and I'll think about letting you reform me," he whispered against her ear.

She turned back on impulse, surprised by the need to comfort him. She was a woman who planned and tried and methodically massaged her life into being livable. Yet there she was, fingers speared into Adam's hair, pulling back the thick, shaggy mass. His eyes narrowed on her, warningly, and yet she kept her hold, studying his face, searching it. The bones were there—high cheekbones, deep-set eyes, those slashing black eyebrows, a nose that wasn't exactly straight and that hard, grim mouth. "You've taken everything from me, Adam. I'm not likely to give more. But I'm not going to be responsible for you disappointing your family. You must not have wanted to open that security box, because you'd left it alone for years. But you did—for Liam—and you brought back a trunk that means so much to the entire family—lost heirlooms and legends. That only made you more dear to them. You're brooding about Sarah, and one day, you'll pick up and run. Now you go to Elspeth's breakfast, and you listen to what they have to say

about those heirlooms. Don't you dare just drop the truth
on Liam and a trunk that holds so many answers and then
swagger away, untouched. Don't run from this, Adam.''

That hot gray look glanced away, avoiding hers. Then it
slashed back again, cold as steel. Each word struck at her.
''I don't run.''

There wasn't a kind line on his face, his mouth pressed
tightly, his gray eyes furious. Anger heated his body, vi-
brating it; the coils of his wrath wrapping around her. But
into her came creeping a softer emotion, one to heal and
gentle. She moved her hands slowly over his face, feeling
those glossy lashes brush her skin, the hard bones beneath
the weathered skin, the stubble of his jaw. He looked down
at her warily as she studied the textures, found them with
her fingertips. There was power there, the set of his jaw,
that pulse beating heavily at his throat—she stroked a fingertip over it and Adam frowned. An incredible sweet sense
of feminine power swept over her, intoxicating her. He
hadn't moved since she'd touched him, as if he were sus-
pended by that light, seeking movements of her hands.

She saw the wary pain inside, felt the ache, and knew
that Adam had trusted few people. He'd been betrayed by
a woman he treasured, the discovery was fresh and warring
within him. ''It won't hurt, you know, to give a little of
yourself to them.''

''I have nothing to give. It isn't there.''

''Find it. You're a hunter. You've dived for treasures off
the coast of Florida, according to the preschool teacher.
And Australia, where you were bitten by a shark. You've
found a boy, separated from his family in a flood. You've
tracked poachers. You've done so much hunting, Adam.
Isn't it time you found what is within yourself? Maybe this
is the place to do it. Maybe you can start all over—right
here. Sam—''

Adam's frown darkened, and then his hands circled her
wrists, taking her hands from him. '''Sam,''' he repeated
flatly.

The word was slashed with frustration, and Adam turned his back to her. He jammed his hands into his jeans' back pockets and braced his legs apart. He looked like a warrior ready to fight; he looked like a lonely man without an anchor.

Jillian found her open hand upon his back, covered by his sweatshirt, the powerful muscles slid beneath her touch. "It will be shearing time right away. The flock isn't that big and it won't take that much work. But meanwhile—"

Adam's body tensed. "You think I'm afraid of work."

Before she could answer, he turned slowly to her. "You're not afraid of me now, are you?"

That question stunned her. They'd been talking about his life and now he returned the probe into her fears. "Well, I—"

He pulled on his old army coat, lighter weight than the peacoat beside it. Above them, on a shelf, the Tallchief plaid and kilt were folded neatly. "Let's just go to Elspeth's and see what she has to say, shall we?"

"Wear the plaid, would you? It means so much to Elspeth."

Adam lifted an eyebrow. "And you? Will you come?"

She didn't answer, because in the last few moments, she didn't know what meant the most to her—revenge and the past, or Adam's tenderness and the tantalizing kisses.

They tasted of a hunger she couldn't afford. Not with Adam.

Six

Excitement danced around Elspeth as she hurried to welcome Adam and Jillian into her home. Sybil and Liam were already in Elspeth's weaving room, seated at the large, rough wooden table. The color skeins of wool, the huge spinning wheel, and shelves of dyes and bags of unspun wool seemed to create the perfect setting for sorting out heritage. Bundles of dried herbs hung from the rafters, scenting the room, while morning slid through the windows to softly drape it in color. Excitement coursed through the usually serene Elspeth as she hurried to her kitchen. "Go right into the weaving room. The tea is in the pot, and I'll bring your breakfast in here. Alek and Duncan have the children at the old place—I think they're constructing a super-duper Sam the Truck highway set— Ah, good! You've worn the plaid, that was thoughtful on a day like today. So did Liam."

When Adam put his hands on Jillian's light coat to remove it, she stiffened. He pushed away the surge of anger that she'd been mishandled and he wasn't on her "trust" list. He pulled it away, aware that Elspeth was watching as she passed with two heaping plates of food. "Jillian was just driving by my place this morning. That's why she was nice enough to give me a ride on her way over here. Wasn't that good of her?" he asked, teasing Jillian.

There was nothing sweet or nice in the stare she shot him.

"You've always given the truth, and nothing less will serve you now, Adam," Elspeth said gently.

He removed his plaid and coat and gave it to Sybil's waiting hands. "I don't know what you mean," he said, aware of Jillian's close look.

"What *do* you mean, Elspeth?" she asked, looking from Elspeth to Adam and back again.

"He's bred to keep his honor and his pride and the truth. He's a Tallchief, and a hunter. He'll find what he seeks, just as he did this chest," Elspeth stated with a smile.

"Elspeth the Elegant," Adam said, teasing her with her childhood name, which he'd learned from her siblings. Then because she seemed oddly a part of him, he bent to kiss her cheek; she gave him a light nudge with her elbow that said she'd grown up with brothers teasing her.

The handcrafted cradle was filled and waiting on the table. Liam shook his head as Adam and Jillian sat next to each other on the bench seats.

"Tea," Liam stated sharply.

He slid a dark look to the large yellow pot on the table and a meaningful frown to the brew in his cup.

"It won't hurt you to have tea this morning, Liam. When we were growing up, my brothers attended my tea parties, and since you've missed your share then, you can have it now," Elspeth said, not at all offended after years of her brothers condemning the brew as "hot water over grass." "It's a special morning, after all, isn't it? To resolve the past and look forward to gentler times?"

"Not everyone wants to revisit the past," Adam stated,

and resented the harshness in his tone. Jillian still thought of him as a liar, the cause of her family's ruin and Tom's death. Adam had just discovered that he loved her this morning, and the clash between the two emotions were certain to bring more pain.

Jillian poured the tea into the waiting cups and handed one to Adam. "Drink."

With its loom and spinning wheel and balls of colored yarn waiting in a basket, its fragrant bundles of herbs hanging from the rafters, the room was a woman's domain and he was clearly under a woman's orders. Adam wrestled with taking orders from anyone, and settled for a long, shuddering sigh; it effectively noted his protest. "Liam should have the cradle," he said.

Jillian nudged him with her elbow, a reminder to wait for a ceremony he didn't understand. "Let's eat first."

"It's so like men to want to hurry through," Sybil said. "But if we're patient and match the journals, Una's and Elizabeth's, to the items in the cradle, we'll be richer for it."

Elspeth had her say. "And you had our husbands down at Maddy's for half the night. Not that we mind, but you do owe us. Most likely we'll be taking it out in baby-sitting."

Adam realized that he had just been given a family tit-for-tat lesson. "Could it be, Elspeth, dear cousin, that I've circled the world, just to be put in my place?"

"Aye. I've no doubt, I'll have to bring you up right, just as I have my brothers. In fact, I've missed the challenge. And the sweet victory."

"Uh." Liam's grunt said he could wait, and his expression said he was still dwelling on Sarah's deceit.

Adam jammed a wedge of pancake into his mouth and chewed while he decided on a comeback for Jillian's earlier elbow nudge reminder—to keep quiet during the sharing of their heirlooms. He settled for a stealthy caress on Jillian's bottom, giving it a gentle pat; his pride eased a bit as he watched her blush rise. When those furious golden eyes lashed at him, he served her his most innocent smile.

He placed the box he'd carried on the center of the table. "Someone gave me something Sarah wanted me to have. You might as well add it to the rest."

"Her things belong only to you," Liam stated. "I want no part of them."

Adam turned to his brother, torn between loving him and defending Sarah.

"It's for you, Adam. From a woman who cared enough to save it for you," Jillian stated.

"Let's begin," Elspeth said, clearing away the plates. "First of all, the cradle is lovely and definitely Tallchief's work, crafted to sell and support his growing family. Those are his marks, and that of a few teething babies."

She studied the dove and the hawk feathers, and nodded to Sybil. She quickly turned the pages of Elizabeth's journal to find a passage. She read, "'Twas no delight that I took in the man who came hunting me. He knew well enough I had secretly borne his son, and he wanted not only the babe, but myself in marriage. I couldn't deny his claim, for my baby wore his mark. 'Twas my penalty for taking Liam as he lay on the new land's mountainous ground, staked there by outlaws, who would have me do the deed to save my sister's life. And so I did, and when the babe came, it was gladly so. That thick black thatch of hair spoke of Tallchief blood, and the gray eyes of Scots, when my own are blue. Aye, that hunter came to England after his child, and me. Later, he hunted more than my body and our child—he came after my heart.'"

Jillian's hand went to her throat. "You mean *she* took *him* against his will? Surely not."

"Aye, she did," Elspeth said with a nod. "It was either that or her sister would die, and herself. She knew their fate would be worse in the outlaws' hands, and she also struck a bargain with their leader for Liam's safety. Elizabeth knew how to challenge and barter…she caught and

held the outlaws' remaining honor. But Liam didn't like a
woman protecting him, let alone taking him. Go ahead,
Sybil. Read.''

Sybil's finger ran down the lovely old script. '' ''When he
forced me to come back to the new land with him, I had
kept with me a dove's feather from my family castle. It was
pure white, as pure as I was before I took Liam, and unlike
the gray birds found here. Then, here, I found a hawk's.
My Liam reminded me of that hawk, so fierce and strong.
Though he was well pleased with his son, he was still furious with me for taking what belonged only to him, for
taking what was his to give, his seed. I would not have our
son know of the strife between us, or how he came to be,
so I gave the feather to Liam as a peace offering.

'' ''He showed me one night by our campfire how the
feathers, so different, suited each other. First by turning
them back to back, as first we slept like that, angry with
each other. Then slowly, with time, the hawk feather turned
to gently curve close to the smaller dove's, a perfect fit.
'Twas a legend his mother, Una, had taught him— The
woman who brings the hawk and the dove feathers to the
hunter shall tame him in gentler ways. He will be her
strength, protecting her, but she has her own powers, most
tender and loving. 'Twill not be easy for the hawk and the
dove, one bred to hunt, and the other of a gentler nature.
Together they grow into each other's lives, and love will
be born.' ''

"That's lovely," Jillian said as Adam brushed a tear
from her cheek with his thumb. "My own family has nothing so lovely."

"They had you," he said firmly, and that quiet statement
shook the room. He couldn't bear not touching her then,
and took her hand for all to see, right there on the table.
His clasp was loose enough that she could remove hers, to
make a choice, and instead Jillian's remained. He searched
the faces around the table and found no surprise to match
his own. "Get on with it."

Who needed more? he wondered as he listened to Sybil's genealogy chart and the new journals there, traced the items from Tallchief and Liam, from the West to Alaska and back again, each carefully pegged with a legend or a story.

When the room was silent, Liam stated firmly, "The cradle is for both of us. I can't keep it filled all the time, Adam. You'll have to do your share."

"I gave up that idea a long time ago."

"Well, pick it up again." Apparently, Adam thought, brothers didn't know how to keep their place.

Jillian glanced at Adam and their hands, locked together in plain sight on the wooden table, and as if realizing the implications, slid hers away.

"Oh, sorry," she said nervously as she rose from the table and hurried to get her coat from the closet. "I've forgotten that I have a conference call with Sam this morning. I have to go. Adam, you're staying, of course," she stated more firmly with a narrowed, meaningful look.

He understood perfectly. Sam wasn't calling this morning. She didn't want Adam near; not only this morning's events lay between them, but she had brought the feathers to him—her enemy. The man she should want to destroy. She was in flight now, fearing what had risen between them and fearing herself. Going after her would not help. Jillian was a private person, and sharing herself caused her to feel endangered. To her, he was danger itself.

He longed to hold her in his arms, but instead nodded. "Thanks for the ride."

"Oh, yes," she answered absently, her face pale. "Goodbye."

Adam turned back to the others and did not shield his mood. "There's something that runs between us," he said simply. "And it's old and not a smooth course."

"Then set one," Liam warned. "She's half in love with Sam already."

"More than half. When she speaks of him, she glows," Adam murmured darkly.

"You'll have to be sweet and understand the journey she must make alone. Today is not tomorrow, but it's not the past, either." Elspeth moved the box with the feathers back to him. "This is yours. All of the legends have proven true so far—Liam's the fire and the flint last of all. Unless you are afraid—"

When Adam leveled a cool look at her, she said lightly, "Let's get on with it, shall we?"

Adam tried to concentrate on the heritage spread in front of him, but his mind was filled with Jillian. She'd been shocked at the tale of how Liam had been staked to the ground, with Elizabeth, the English lady, taking him without his permission.

If that had shocked her, Adam's restless dreams of Jillian pouring herself over him, would have— He met Elspeth's gaze, the wisdom of it, and knew that loving Jillian would be no simple journey. Not with the past and Sam standing between them. He'd fought a town with the truth, and had lost that when he wanted a woman. It was best that he told her soon.

What could he say? "Jillian, I'm really Sam. I wanted to keep you here, and so I arranged work for you."

He shook his head. Now, that would raise her self-image, wouldn't it? A man hiring her because he wanted her and not her skills. She was good, just starting out in a life she wanted, and—

Adam shook his head. He couldn't hurt her that way. He'd think of something else. Meanwhile, his personal tension had made him snap at Steve, and he'd regretted it instantly. He'd apologized, but he couldn't allow others to suffer for his torn emotions and sleepless nights. Deception hadn't ever been his game, nor had the hunger that pursued him every moment. He hadn't planned to fall in love, but there it was, just like the chest and Sarah's secret.

He didn't notice Liam pouring more tea into his cup, and didn't notice the taste as he drank. Instead, he lifted an ornate beaded band and studied it, running his thumb across the sky-blue beads. He thought of how it would look over Jillian's gleaming auburn hair and sipped more tea and tasted her kiss once more. He had tasted a fusion of needs, man and woman, as if everything else had been placed aside, including the past.

When Liam laughed out loud, Adam blinked. He swung back to the reality of Elspeth's home and noted that it was tea in his cup and Liam was to blame. He had planned to leave everything to his brother, but he wanted to give Jillian something of family, his family and his heritage. "If Liam is in agreement, I think we should share our parents' things, and the rest with all the other Tallchiefs—maybe keeping it safe and researching it for the others. But if it makes no difference to anyone, I've got a use for this," he said quietly.

Elspeth and Liam nodded. "Give it to her, and soon," Elspeth offered. "And be prepared for the consequences. That headband was meant for courting a woman."

That night, Jillian arranged one layer of her advertising design closer to the other, and electronically brought one layer from the back to the front. Each layer held an image of Sam the Truck's friends, but Nancy was featured, the collage for the side of the box beginning to take shape as Jillian sized and adjusted the colors and shadows. She worked from other artists' work: the developers of Tracy, the Pickup Truck and Eddie the Railroad Crossing Warning with his long black-and-white arm.

Jillian took the image of Nancy and curved it slightly, giving the toy an animated look. She stared at the computer screen. If only life could be that easy, to move what didn't suit you to the background, to crop off the edges you didn't want, to arrange what happened to you as you wanted.

She opened the small box with the silver ring Adam had given her a long time ago. While he'd slept that morning, he'd looked younger, but his raw sexuality had caught her.

She longed to smooth that strand of hair back from his forehead, to trace a fingertip over those sleek black brows.

Jillian scrubbed her face with her hands. How could she possibly want Adam? Yet her body had heated and hungered, just by looking at him, by following that masculine line of his chest, that flat stomach, the way his shorts slid a little low on one side where the skin should have paled and didn't.

Then he'd stirred, and fearing that one sleepy, sensual look would cause her to ease down into his arms, she'd geared up her temper and doused him with water. Jillian shook her head. She had never done anything so rash. She was a predictable woman without primitive urges to—

Those feathers. That legend. Her hands shook and she clasped them together as she thought of how Adam could make her *feel.* Angry. More than that, furious. An emotion she never allowed herself. What made her catch that thick hair and pull it back from his face to study all the arrogance, the textures, those searing, thunderous gray eyes?

The gesture was too primitive, unlike Jillian Green O'Malley's calm, methodical ones. She'd taken steps to create a new life, but she was always in control. Jillian struggled to place the legend of the feathers in perspective—true, she'd brought the feathers to Adam, but she'd only obeyed a dying woman's request, nothing more.

Yet, the legend born with so many of the Tallchief family's stood firm in her mind. *The woman who brings the hawk and the dove feathers to the hunter shall tame him in gentler ways. He will be her strength, protecting her, but she has her own powers, most tender and loving. 'Twill not be easy for the hawk and the dove, one bred to hunt and the other of a gentler nature. Together they grow into each other's lives, and love will be born.*

Jillian did not feel gentle where Adam was concerned. She shivered as she thought of Elizabeth Montclair, separated from her hunting party in the mountains. The Englishwoman had taken an unwilling man, staked to the ground, and had saved her life and her sister's. As a result, she'd had his son, after returning to England. And then Liam Tallchief had come after her. In the end, she'd loved him. Life certainly hadn't been arranged to Elizabeth's liking, certainly not at first, and she had been his unwilling bride.

Jillian frowned slightly; she knew a bit about being an unwilling bride, and nothing of love. In her mind, she saw Adam's hand joined with hers, the strength holding her gently. She tasted again his raw, hungry kiss as she ran a fingertip across her lips.

On impulse, she picked up the telephone and dialed Adam's number. "Adam," he answered, as if distracted.

She wanted to tell him to put no trust in the legend, that love wasn't brewing between them. She wasn't a romantic; she functioned on what she had to do to survive— "Jillian?" he asked after a moment.

She cleared her throat. "It was difficult for you today, and for Liam. But you did it. And it meant so much to the others that you stayed. I'm sorry that I woke you up like that—"

"I'm not. Jillian, there is something I have to tell you—"

"You're free to go, if you wish," she hurried on, her thoughts confused as she heard a noise. "What's that? It sounds electronic."

"Hmm? Oh, that must be the bed creaking."

Adam in bed. Jillian swallowed as she remembered how he had looked, how she'd wanted to reach out and sweep her hand over that broad chest, to feel the texture of it, skin and hair, and trail her finger down that line flowing lower....

"Don't worry about me, Adam," she said finally, as she struggled for logic.

"What's wrong, Jillian?"

She wanted him to hold her as a woman, to feel that strength and heat and desire. "I've got to get back to work," she said, and hung up.

It took moments to remove her shaking hand from the telephone, to accept that she had just called Adam, her enemy. It took more time for her to stand and shake her head. On her feet and stalking the small room back and forth, Jillian threw up her hands. She picked up a pillow and hurled it without direction. It hit her philodendron and knocked it to the floor. On its way, it brushed a small lamp, which also tumbled.

"I have no idea why I called him. None at all. Absolutely pointless. There's nothing between us. Men are naturally aroused in the morning, and well, there I was. He's got me all mixed up. He's out to make trouble for me, that's it. He's out to make trouble, some sort of weird male payback. He wants to unnerve me, and he knows just how to do it. I came here for revenge, to destroy him, and I'm kissing him? Why, Jillian? Why would you let *him* kiss you?"

A small noise behind her caused Jillian to pivot. Adam stood at the door, his arms crossed, his head tilted. His voice was deep and slow and sensual. "Because you liked it? Because I definitely liked it?"

"What are you doing here?"

"From the sound of your voice I thought you might need help somehow. And I wanted to see you."

Adam's slow, flickering gaze was taking in the T-shirt she wore, the length of her legs. The thin material did little to shield her breasts, and Jillian crossed her arms over them. "You sleep in that now, do you?" he asked in that deep, raw tone that slid to quiver and warm and heat inside her.

She couldn't move as he walked toward her. In his open hand was a leather strip, intricately and beautifully beaded. He tied the end thongs around her forehead. "This was Elizabeth's, a gift from her mother-in-law, Una. It was meant to give her courage and strength to make a life as she wished—with or without Liam. To make her choices. He wouldn't have held her forever, and in the end, she chose him."

Jillian's fingers traced the brilliant blue beading. The

smooth texture in contrast to the rougher doeskin delighted her. "This belongs to you. I can't take it."

Adam's hand cruised her cheek, his thumb caressing it. He leaned down to whisper unevenly, "Take me as I am, Jillian. Let the past go. Enjoy what we can have—an understanding that we've both had trials and we've survived and here we are, a man and a woman. Just that—a man and a woman."

"You make me unpredictable. I do not have a temper, Adam, and yet you bring it right out of me."

His thumb stroked the sensitive corner of her lips. "And other things, as well. I held a woman in my arms this morning. Full of heat and passion, hungry for life."

"You're mistaken." She'd thought of herself as cold for years, yet—

"Let's try it again, just to make certain," he said, and slowly bent his lips to hers.

The heat and the hunger lingered on each brush of his lips upon hers, tantalizing, asking, offering. "Jillian..." he whispered in a tone that matched the aching of her body.

He took her hand and placed it over his heart, pressing his own over hers. The kisses teased and warmed and stirred, until Jillian had to move closer. Adam's arms came around her, his hands opened on her upper back and lower, pressing her against him. He breathed unsteadily, a great ragged sigh passing through him, as if he had come through forever to stand and hold her like this.

She'd never felt so safe, so wanted. "I'm not afraid of you, Adam," she whispered.

His lips caused her to shiver as they roamed her throat and curved into a smile against her skin.

"You're not, love? That's good."

"Are you afraid of me?" she asked, unexpectedly teasing him, and followed the urge to nip gently at his throat.

"Yes, I am," he said fervently, raggedly. "You tear something from me that is too sweet for words."

Then his hands began to move, slowly, thoroughly, and

Jillian waited for each caress, pleasured until she began to enjoy the shape and heat of his body, his shoulders, the cords and muscles moving in his arms. She realized distantly that he had turned off the lights. His hands flowed beneath her T-shirt now, smoothing, tempting, light and gentle, despite the rough calluses. She didn't protest as he eased it from her, curiosity driving her, wanting to see how he looked at her body, how he touched it so gently. Adam's intimacy was new and gentle and safe, as if she were flowing down a warm sunlit stream.

Her mind told her to take this bit, this one moment when a man touched her gently, waiting for her to stop him before moving on. The gentle seeking brought her no terror, only pleasure, and she would have this at least to remember in the cold years to come—one warm lovely image to erase all the others.

She swam in wonderful, delightful textures, in pleasure that kept rising higher. "Adam—"

"Say my name again like that, as if you needed me, wanted me."

"Adam—"

This time his kiss seared, slanted against her lips, his tongue tempting hers. But his wasn't the savage need tearing free, igniting out of control. Jillian pressed closer, feeding upon tastes, small mysterious explosions of danger and safety mixed, of the future, of heat and storm, and the incredible sense of being fearless, dominant, wild, feminine, desired and very, very hungry for more.

He groaned deep in his throat, echoing that hunger, and Jillian's hands gripped his hair, tethering him to those primitive, wild kisses. He shuddered against her, and his hand searched for her breast. She hadn't expected the delight of being treasured as he cupped her breast. But the shock of his mouth, warm and sucking, tore free needs and hungers she hadn't known she possessed, staking her to that one moment. *Adam.*

She'd waited so long to feel like this, free and strong and alive and blooming inside—*Adam.*

His hands ran over her possessively, firmly now, seeking her breasts, her waist, then dug into the flare of her hips, tugging her tight against the hardness that nestled between her thighs, separated by layers of cloth.

She was almost a part of him, fearless, hungry, a counterpart to the flow of his hard, powerful body. She knew the mechanics of sex, and yet with Adam, she longed for him to fill her, to complete her.

With a harsh groan, Adam wrapped his arms around her and lifted her. "Jillian...Jillian, we have to stop."

Then he looked down at her breasts, rounded and pressed against him, and shook his head as he lowered her feet to the floor.

Jillian leaned against him, her legs unsteady. She couldn't face him and rested her cheek against the hard racing of his heart. Adam stroked her hair, rocking her against his body. "You haven't done anything wrong, Jillian. Shh."

The evidence of his body said he still wanted her, and yet, he'd stopped. Jillian shuddered, remembering a man who hadn't.

"I'm not him, Jillian." Again, Adam had stepped into her mind and noted that special fear.

She wanted Adam to keep holding her so she would feel just like that—protected, warm, comforted—forever. She lifted her face to study his, the lines more fierce now, honed and stark, his hair rumpled by her fists—

She'd clutched his hair in her fist, holding him to their kiss, taking greedily.

She took in the power of his shoulders, taut with desire that he withheld, the rapid pulse of his throat.... Her eyes widened—there were small marks there, made by her teeth nibbling on him.

"Oh, my," she said as Adam pulled an afghan around her, easing her away and into the small rocker.

He rammed his fingers through his hair and studied her darkly. Then, as if needing something to do and fearing to leave her alone, Adam picked up the fallen lamp and straightened it. In the shadows, he moved to clean up the dirt and the plant, and then he sat on a chair, staring off into the night.

She couldn't bear to look at him; he seemed so lonely, so hard and untouchable, so isolated. The need to soothe him moved through her, where once a more primitive urge ruled. She wanted to hold him, this time as a friend.

The creaking of her rocking chair echoed through the room. She sensed that he was staying for her, to see if she could cope with what she'd found between them, or if she'd start blaming him. "I'm all right. You can go now," she whispered to free him from whatever he brooded.

"Fine," he said curtly, and stood.

On his way to the door, Adam bent close to her and took her hand. He pressed his face within her palm, nuzzling it, and she sensed a loneliness that had nothing to do with his previous hunger. When he lifted his head, his eyes were gentle upon her, taking in the headband, her flushed face and the way she gripped the afghan around her.

After he had gone, Jillian sat rocking for a long time. She couldn't find the hatred that had driven her family and herself. How could she trust him and feel so safe with him? Could all those years have changed him? Or her?

It was no gentle urge that moved through her when he kissed her, that was for certain.

How could she separate her body and her heart and her mind? Trust for Adam lay in her heart and her body, but her mind replayed all those scenes and pain years ago. Had she betrayed her parents? Her brother?

Could Adam possibly have told the truth all those years ago?

Jillian used the edge of the afghan to wipe away the tears streaming down her face. *She'd wanted Adam desperately.* All those empty, painful years lodged in her chest, waging against the desire Adam had just ignited in her. None of it made sense, the layers tearing away until nothing existed but Adam and herself.

Yet part of her hungered for the tenderness and the safety and the passion that she'd found with Adam. She went to lie on her bed, pulling the afghan around her and staring at the moonlight sliding through the windows.

Whatever she'd tasted with Adam, it wasn't hatred. It was alive and hungry and happy...and she feared what it might bring.

He still tasted her.

Adam stood near Tallchief Lake, overlooking the brooding waters that matched his own dark mood.

An hour after holding her, his body still throbbed with the need to lay Jillian down on that old-fashioned bed and to make love with her.

Without the past resolved, it could have been a disfavor to them both.

He'd have been making love to a woman who thought he'd ruined her family, who thought he'd lied. His pride and honor demanded more than that momentary satisfaction. He needed her to believe in him, to believe he told the truth long ago.

She could settle that need to hunt for peace—she was his peace, soft and warm and soothing. Was that what he was doing all these years, filling them with motion so that he didn't have to think about the girl, and now the woman?

There was more to Jillian than she knew, more woman and heart. Giving came naturally to her; he'd seen it with each touch she gave a child. With the smile that came from her heart.

The waves lapped against the reeds near the bank, and Adam thought of how his relatives brought their brides here, in tepees for their honeymoon. Strange how he should want what others had had, the courting and the ceremony, the legends—

Was this what he had hunted for? he asked himself again. Home, peace and the comfort of a special woman?

She didn't believe him and she couldn't let the past go. Neither could he accept less.

He lifted his face to the cold wind and watched the moon, waited for it to call to him, to tell him it was time to go.

But it wasn't. It was time to stand and fight. How? What did he know of giving love, or tending a woman with a gentle, but damaged heart?

Wait, the wind whistled through the swaying reeds.

He tossed a stick out into the water. "For what? For her to find out that I'm Sam? I should have told her tonight. But I didn't. So much for courage."

Wait, the wind returned. *Stay true to what is right.*

What was true is that he'd been just as shaken as Jillian. He needed her in the tenderest of ways, he needed to love her and to be loved in return. And he needed to tell her the truth.

Seven

Late the next morning, Jillian couldn't concentrate on her work, and sitting at Elspeth's giant loom gave her a peace she badly needed. The house was quiet now, scented of Elspeth's bread, the Petrovnas shopping at the feed store for their garden seeds. It was a grand family occasion, the careful selection of seeds, while the pumpkin seeds from last year's garden rested in a pottery bowl on the big wooden table. The garden-planting tradition was no small activity, Elspeth had explained; she wanted to share with her children what she had had with her parents. It wasn't considered work, but more of sharing and providing and giving a sense of passing on what had been given.

The old cradle, still filled with heirlooms, sat in the corner. Liam refused to take anything but one small present for his wife and another for his son. He wanted his brother to help make the decisions, and Adam wasn't budging. Elspeth had said it was a hard time for the brothers, Adam

was trying to forgive Sarah, while Liam's feelings ran
harsh.

In the shadowy silence, Jillian had found more peace and
sense than she had in her lifetime. Out in the Petrovna
garden, just tilled and softened, a meadowlark trilled mu-
sically and the house was filled with silent, warm echoes
of children playing, Alek laughing and Elspeth's knowing,
loving ways.

Jillian's own home had been based on status possessions,
hosting parties, belonging to the right set. Love wasn't an
element. Nor was trust.

She cruised the shuttle through the wool again. With
each thought, she brought down the beater-bar to push the
yarn tighter against the already-woven length.

Every instinct she had told her that Adam hadn't lied all
those years ago. Another man might have taken advantage
of her last night, her passion ruling her. But then her passion had never ruled her, had it? Or love of anyone, but
her family?

Questioning the past years brought her nothing but con-
fusion. Her parents had been adamant that Adam had lied
to get back at Tom. For what reason? Adam was the high
school's leading student and athlete, while Tom barely
scraped through the courses.

Tom. What did she remember of him? She had believed
her parents without question. *She'd never questioned, not
as a girl. As a woman, she wanted to know more.*

Kevin, her husband. He'd wanted the passion she'd felt
with Adam, and yet Jillian couldn't respond to Kevin in
that earthshaking way.

Herself. She wove a vermillion stripe across the dragon-
green, the symbol of Tallchief entering the ancient Scots
plaid. She'd just discovered a temper that Adam could ignite, and the passion to go with it, the need to consume and
to take. There was no calm, safe distance when she was
near Adam, no protection against herself. A woman used

to giving—in fact, she'd given her life to hating Adam—Jillian wasn't used to her own greed, her own hungers.

Why did her instincts tell her to trust Adam? That would falsify a lifetime of believing the damage he'd done.

Why did she want to soothe the ache that she sensed in him?

She glanced out at the fence where buttery daffodils were lined against the old gray posts. Her mother had ordered florist-cut flowers. The arrangement was no more lovely that the daffodils on Elspeth's table, an old fruit jar serving as a container instead of cut glass.

Jillian wove blue yarn, in and out, across the dragon-green pattern, and brought down the beater-bar. She'd been a girl trying to please parents who couldn't be satisfied, and now she was a woman trying to untangle the past. How many women had sorted their thoughts while seated at a loom? she wondered, running her hand across the new Tallchief plaid that Elspeth had started.

At a sound, she saw Adam lean his shoulder against the door. The shadows did not soften his rugged look, the wind-tossed hair, the black sweatshirt and faded jeans, the workman's battered boots. He nodded a solemn greeting to her and lifted the thick wedge of buttered bread. "I borrowed the tractor and plow for Liam's new garden place, and I'm returning it. Elspeth said to come in and get my share of her bread and to stay to help plant their garden later."

Adam settled on a wooden bench near the wall, his long legs extended. "It's a good home, isn't it?"

"The very best." This morning, she could find no anger for Adam, only the soft need to have him near. From his troubled glance at the cradle, she wondered if he didn't need her, too; someone from the past who knew how deep his pain had cut. "Sarah was a lovely woman. Liam will come to understand."

"Don't let me disturb you." Clearly, Adam didn't want to talk about Sarah's deceit, or Liam's rage.

Jillian nodded and returned to her weaving and her thoughts. Companionship wasn't what she expected of Adam, but that was what she felt circling her, the warmth of a friend, one who was solid and honorable and good.

Strange that she would feel about Adam like that. "I can't remember Tom anymore," she said, sliding the shuttle through the weave. "All I can remember are feelings—unclear bitter images, and fear for my family."

He didn't speak and, glancing at his face, she found sorrow. He looked down at his hands, rubbed them together as if he were forming a thought, and then shook his head.

What troubled him so? Was it the loss of Sarah? Or her secret, harbored too long? Or was it Liam, storming and hurt by her deceit? After just meeting his brother, Adam was already torn between him and memories of Sarah.

Why should Jillian ache to smooth his hair? To hold him close?

She continued to weave as Adam sat in the shadows, and the sense that she wasn't alone curled around her, peacefully. She had no idea how much time had passed with Adam sitting still, watching her as she wove. Whatever primitive passion had ruled them last night, calm wove between them now—they were people who had shared a past and who knew more about each other than anyone else.

Then the Petrovna pickup pulled into the ranch yard and Alek was laughing with the children. As Jillian looked outside the window, she noted Elspeth standing absolutely still, staring at the weaving room. "I could use some of Elspeth's ability to understand," Jillian said softly.

"It's a good place for thinking," Adam said quietly.

"Tell me what you think."

He shook his head and stood. "It's for you to do the sorting. I already know."

"Know what?"

But Adam was walking out into the daylight, already lifting a child upon his shoulders as if he'd always been a part of the Tallchiefs. When Jillian came outside, she felt like an outsider, unprepared for the excitement of a farming family about their garden.

Alek and Adam were already busy with the tilled ground, using stakes and thread strung between them to set the lines for beans and corn. The deep male voices rumbled over the bright April day, and Adam called to Jillian. "You need some fresh air. Don't just stand there. Come help."

"Me? I have no idea about gardening." Gardeners had tended her family lawns and plants, then later on, struggling for her independence, she hadn't had time for anything more than a few houseplants.

"Time to learn. If you're not afraid of getting your hands dirty." With experience, Adam crouched to scoop up the soil, to feel and study it, and she wondered how many crops he had helped tend, in how many lands. They had lived in two separate worlds, and now there was only sunshine and his challenge to get her hands dirty. It all seemed so simple.

In the end, Jillian enjoyed herself. With the official title of "seed dropper," she was to place three seeds in each hole. When the garden was planted, Adam looked across it and grinned at her. The warmth sailed across the fresh April air and caught her, bringing her own heady sense of lightness and right.

"I'm going to look at a beauty of a pickup. Want to come along?" He studied her with those cool gray eyes and that tilt to his head, as if he didn't expect her to accept.

She stared at her nails, garden dirt beneath the short length. She'd played classical piano, not with sand and mudpies, and now— The lash of her mother's scolding cut into her, and she tossed the echo away into the April sunshine. She wasn't a girl any longer and yet, she felt new and clean and so incredibly strong. It was a day to savor, to experience whatever life tossed at her.

It had tossed her her first tractor ride, sitting on Adam's lap as she'd driven across a wide, rolling field, the cattle staring at the intrusion. She'd learned to shift gears and clutch and gas, according to his directions, his hand firmly

over hers. Delighted with the novel experience, Jillian had
laughed out loud.

Adam's hand had turned her face slowly to his. He'd
eased away the strands that the wind had pushed against
her face. "That sounds good—you laughing."

"I feel good. Capable, in charge," she'd mocked herself
with a grin. "I love this. I don't know why."

"Just don't charge over that fence." That time his kiss
was light and gentle, catching the sunlight and her happiness and giving it back to her.

Jillian forced herself away from Adam's searching gaze,
from the friendship she felt tangling with something deeper.
The easy caress of his hand on her back said he was a man
who enjoyed touching her.

The "beauty" Adam was considering purchasing—a
dented, rusty, blue 50's Ford pickup—stood inside a weathered barn. Chickens had roosted in the back, and when
checking beneath the hood, Adam removed a mouse nest.
He and the farmer who wanted to sell it, quickly dealt with
the cobwebs.

The old farmer peered at her. "You can have my mis-
sus's canning jars in the back of the pickup with the deal.
She's not doing that anymore and she said if Adam's girlfriend looked like the loving kind to give them to you.
Passing on canning jars means something hereabouts. You
look like a nice couple, one of those fierce Tallchief boys
and a soft woman to tame him. They're yours, if you want
them. The wife and me are all packed and moving out to
Las Vegas to be with our grandchildren."

Jillian glanced at the cardboard box filled with jars, some
of them blue with age, some with zinc lids. They were
lovely and almost seemed to glow softly with another
woman's tending. She ignored the "girlfriend" remark; it
mattered little. She was just here with Adam, having a nice
day. "Thank you. I'd love to have them."

"Get in and start it, Jillian," Adam said, and she stood

still, locked by his confidence in her. She'd driven automatic shifts and had taken buses and metros, but the pickup had a starter button and clutch and gas pedals. At her helpless look, Adam nudged her aside and slid into the seat, starting the motor. With a hurried kiss and a grin, he was gone and the old pickup truck was rumbling around her, and Adam was bending beneath the hood.

"Rev it up," he called, and when she did, he and the farmer toyed with adjustments, the pickup truck shuddering and roaring in the old barn. Jillian held on to the worn steering wheel and wondered why she was enjoying herself, smiling at Adam when he raised his head to grin at her. He had that little-boy look, delighted with a new toy.

In the end, he wrote a check and shook hands with the farmer, who was clearly losing his beloved. Adam grinned at Jillian, who stood beside him, stunned at the men's language. "She's a little sweetheart. Treat her right. She's got heart."

Adam looked down at her. "I'll get Alek's tractor back to him later. Do you want to drive, or do you want me to?"

"It's your pickup. You drive."

Adam ran a caressing hand over the pickup door. "Jillian. Don't be difficult or polite. Do you want to drive this beauty or not?"

While Adam used the cleaning towel the farmer had given him, Jillian considered the cracked dashboard, the ancient gearshift, the missing windshield wiper and the one that was stuck in the center of the glass. "Beauty" coughed and sputtered all the while, shaking as though she'd die at any time. "You drive."

So there Jillian was, in a rusty, dented, aged pickup with Adam driving and whistling, and caressing the steering wheel and gearshift. The country lane was bumpy with weeds in the center, and Adam proudly noted how the pickup "purred."

Then he slid the old pickup into a grove of trees off the road and turned off the engine. The vehicle sputtered,

coughed and died. Adam turned to her. "I have something
to tell you," he murmured.

But just then, the pickup burped once more as if struggling to run again, and Jillian couldn't help laughing. "Yes,
she's a beauty all right."

Adam scowled at her, clearly taking offense. "Well, she
is. I'll have her purring in no time—she just needs a little
loving and—"

He turned slowly to her with that dark hungry look, and
she knew that he wanted to hold her. "Come here," he
ordered softly.

"Why?" she asked, and wondered at the excitement in
her. She *knew*. Suddenly she was that girl again, alive, love
dancing around her when Adam looked at her. But this time
he was a man and she was a woman who knew the consequences of coming too close, and she'd already tasted
that burning fever.

There in the shadows of the old pickup truck with its
creaks and groans, Adam's hand tilted her face for his long,
slow, seeking kiss. Its sweetness twisted through her, and
with his arm around her now, she lifted her arms to draw
him close, tethering that wild mane in her fists.

The kiss changed, slanted, fused and the storm of hunger
circled her once more. Adam lifted her on his lap and nuzzled her cheeks, her throat, and kissed a lower path while
caressing her breasts. "Jillian," he whispered as she slid
her hand up inside his sweatshirt, smoothing the scars the
shark had given him, the one across his arm.

She loved touching him, the contrast of smooth warm
skin with muscles and cords flowing beneath, the roughness
of flat nipples etching her palm, the tight flat stomach, the
way his navel—

He shuddered at that light, curious touch, his breath ragged. Watching her, Adam slowly pulled off his sweatshirt
and his hands slid to her waist. She nodded in answer to
his silent question, and he pulled away her cardigan and
unbuttoned her blouse.

His hands and eyes treasured her, and her fear did not come. Not even when he lifted her, slid open her jeans, and caressed her softly, intimately. She met the rhythm, cruised in it, floated in pleasure.

From nowhere the storm came and slammed into her, hot, hungry, almost savage in its demand. Whatever had become soft and willing, gently changed, and pulsed and pleasured, growing until it exploded, tossing her against him. The deep vibrations went on beyond her control, gradually diminishing until she lay limply against Adam.

"Oh, Jillian," he murmured against her lips, his body shaking and hard against her.

"Take me somewhere," she whispered urgently, wanting more, all of him, inside her. She wanted him to cleanse away the other times, far less sweet and fulfilling. "Love me."

He shook his head and rocked her. His expression was a mixture of sensual hunger and sorrow and frustration. On the road some distance away, a car drove by, and Adam said quietly, "Let me help you dress."

When she sat beside him again, and the old pickup rumbled down the bumpy farm road, Adam slid his arm around her to pull her close. She sensed that he needed her, that there were things he wanted to say. "What is it, Adam? What troubles you? Sarah?"

She couldn't help lifting to kiss his cheek and then Adam's gray eyes slashed at her in surprise. His expression changed, opened to her, and she saw again the pain that had been there for so many years. He'd been a boy then, accused of lying, rigid with pride. "You give me peace, Jillian, and that is a hard commodity to find. I've hunted it in more lands than I can count. It's no small thing to have that gift—to bring peace to someone else."

She brought him more than peace, Adam brooded that night as he studied the images Steve had sent him on the computer. Jillian's style was there—animated, flowing, eye-catching.

He wanted her, his body humming with desire. Yet she'd regret an impulsive loving later, when she discovered that he was Sam.

What she believed was a lie hovered between them. Adam rammed his hand through his hair and struggled with his options, to leave or to stay, to tell everything and lose, or to hope that— *Hope.* How many times had he tossed that dream away? He'd hoped she'd believe him, and not her brother, all those years ago.

Adam shook his head and damned himself for not telling her the truth, for letting his need for her consume him too soon—

Jillian studied the jars, washed and lined up on her counter. They were beautiful, and she could imagine them standing filled with jams, peaches and green beans in a pantry—what a pretty image. Washing them had given her something to do, because she couldn't concentrate on her Sam projects.

Thinking about Adam's hunger left little room for that. The images of the day rushed by her, Adam sitting as she wove, the quiet peace between them. The gardening and the tractor ride, the way he chuckled when she struggled for control of the big beast—the way he touched her gently, pulling her hair from her face for a kiss. She smiled, remembering his excitement over the "beauty," that boyish grin at her catching her heart, holding it.

Then later, her riveting need for him had shaken her, her body still restless. Was he feeling the same? Was he aching for her? Thinking of her?

It had only taken weeks for her plan of revenge to turn to one of trust. *Why did her instincts tell her that Adam could be trusted? How could she possibly question what her parents had told her? Nothing in the newspapers or the gossip supported his accusation against Tom.*

She smoothed the beads on the headband and carefully tied it around her forehead. Her hand flowed over her breasts, remembering his caresses, the heat of his mouth.

Strange that she had always been so clinical about choosing her life, those people around her, always so safe. Adam wasn't a safe man, not to her—he brought out emotions too wild and fierce, and that odd urge to soothe him.

Jillian turned on her computer and only slightly mourned the time she'd lost during the day—actually living, enjoying herself. She stared at Nancy's colorful package design, and knew that if she stepped back into the past, pain waited. She shouldn't even think about reopening the bitterness, but she wondered how she would see the events now as an adult.

She saw Adam's harsh expression, those gray eyes flashing, his young face set and rigid with anger and pain. He'd wanted her to believe him.

With a sigh, Jillian braced herself and began to hunt through old newspaper archives available through her computer. She couldn't find anything, except the obituaries of her brother and parents, and the auction of the house and furnishings.

The house. A Southern-style mansion had been built to make a statement that the Greens came from wealth and power, that they ranked in the town's very best social circle—or higher. It had been filled with florists' flowers, designer furniture and custom decor, and it was as cold as the crystal that glittered throughout. Completely absorbed in her own world as a society leader, Martha Green had never washed dishes or scrubbed floors. Maxwell Green had never dirtied his hands on an old truck engine or changed a tire. He wouldn't think of manual labor, not even if a friend needed him.

Jillian wrapped her arms around herself and rubbed them. Despite the warmth of her home, the past's chill swept over her. As a woman, she couldn't imagine leaving a little girl alone in a big house for the night. Oh, she'd been locked in the room, of course, a very pretty room where dolls that showed any loving wear were thrown away.

Nothing in Tom's obituary indicated that he had died in prison. In fact, the news at the time had nothing to say of car thefts or of the elderly woman dying, except for her obituary. Yet at the same time in Jillian's home, the bitterness against "that Tallchief boy" had raged incessantly. The absence of any newspaper article on a trial that had Jillian's parents in an uproar—and their friends—seemed strange.

Jillian rummaged through old papers and found the telephone number she wanted. Maude Lanford had been a young court stenographer, a single mother raising three children by herself. She had been a friend to Adam's aunt Sarah, and Jillian had baby-sat for her children more than once. During the trial, Maude had seemed sad and frightened, and she'd avoided Jillian. Why?

Maude answered the call, her voice older, a little cracked and tired. But upon hearing Jillian's name, she brightened. "Jillian? Jillian Green? Hush, now, children. Grandma's on the telephone. Shh. Jillian—I'm so glad you called. How are you? I've thought about you so much. You were always in my prayers."

After a brief conversation, catching up on Maude's second marriage, a happy one, and the marriages of her children, Maude said, "I'm so sorry your marriage didn't work out. But to tell you the truth, I never liked that boy. I felt that your parents pushed you at him after their businesses started to fail—they had to buy off so many people, all the parents of those boys had so many legal fees and debts. Heavens—oh, dear, you didn't know that, did you? I shouldn't have said anything. But they ruined that Tallchief boy's life, and truly put Sarah in an early grave."

Buy off so many people, all the parents of those boys had so many legal fees... Jillian gripped the telephone. "Maude, it is really important that you tell me what went on during that trial, from your point of view."

"The records were sealed. I can't—well, yes, I can. I'm an old woman, but my memory is clear as a bell on that— it was so wrong, and I don't care anymore. Someone should have stood up for that boy, and for Sarah. At the time, I wanted to help, but I was like everyone else—terrified of losing my job. Those families were so powerful, owning all the businesses, controlling everything. All of us were afraid. Sarah's heart was bad and the pressure on her was incredible, the telephone threats, the way she was ostracized. She stood by Adam though, and told him to stand up for what he knew was right."

"I've met him again, and I know that what happened then affected my whole life—and his. I have to resolve this, Maude. Please—"

After the telephone call ended, Jillian sat very still, bombarded by Maude's facts, facts that had never made the local newspaper—the boys' parents were to repay any damage they had done and there were other penalties, such as work programs and not associating with each other outside of school events. The other boys involved had all given testimony against Tom, saying they feared him and that they'd evidenced his brutality.

The prominent families had banded together, shutting down the case, and the judge's sympathy allowed them to go on in life without records. Adam's testimony against Tom proved that the elderly woman had been assaulted and robbed. Then, while awaiting the judge's decision of Tom's additional punishment, he had attacked Adam—and this time there were witnesses. He was sentenced to prison, but the town's elite wasn't letting Adam or Sarah lead a normal life—they were cast out.

Maude's story supported Adam. She'd mentioned too many dates and facts, still clear in her mind, for her to have erred. She remembered the cars that had been stolen, and Jillian remembered how Tom had admired them, watching them hungrily. All the facts fit together. Adam hadn't lied all those years ago. Jillian's parents and Tom had brought about their own ruin.

It was hours before she recovered, her computer still humming as it was before she'd placed the call to Maude. She'd moved from one lifetime to another, from the girl to the woman, understanding the hardships and the facts. Outside the sky was light gray, preceding dawn. It slipped through the window to stir the shadows. Methodically, Jillian turned off her computer. Shaking and numb, she knew what she had to do. She untied the headband and placed it on her desk. She pulled out the silver ring Adam had given her long ago and, still numb, drove to his house.

At dawn, Adam was saddling a horse borrowed from Duncan Tallchief. The night had been too restless to concentrate on work and Jillian filled his mind, the hunger for her haunting him.

He'd hunted in his lifetime, and now he was the hunted—by his conscience, by Jillian's belief of Tom's lie, by the way she looked yesterday, happy and carefree…and by the way she ignited in his arms.

He was greedy, after all, wanting a few moments with her that weren't draped in bitterness. But truth—his Sam deceit—was going to hurt and anger her. Was it wrong to want just that bit of time with her?

He tightened a cinch and traced Jillian's SUV racing toward his house, a silver streak in the dawn. When she braked too quickly, the tires squalled and the vehicle slid sideways. Then she was out the door and hurrying toward him without a coat and wearing the same clothes she had worn yesterday.

"Jillian?" he asked as she shivered, gripped her arms and moved restlessly in front of him. The pink dawn caught the tears streaking her face. "What is it?"

She shook her head, her lips moving as she looked away from him. When she turned back, her expression was incredibly sad. Yet the composure was there, the lady and

the class. "It's a nice morning, isn't it?" she asked unsteadily. "Going for a ride?"

Adam removed his coat and placed it around her shoulders. If she'd discovered he was Sam, he didn't blame her
for hating him. He'd just as soon have the truth now, hard
and fast. He had no excuses, except the real one that he
wanted to know her better. "You didn't come here for conversation. Spell it out."

She shook her head and shivered again. "I can't. I can't
talk about it just yet. I...I don't suppose you'd take me
with you, would you?"

"I'm going camping on Tallchief Mountain—overnight," he added so she would understand that they would
be alone together.

"I... That would be lovely. Just please, please don't talk
now. Just take me someplace, away from here. Away from
everything."

Adam eased her hair back from her face and knew that
whatever she asked, he would do. She wasn't dressed properly, wearing light canvas shoes instead of boots, and the
shadows beneath her eyes said she hadn't slept at all. He'd
need extra clothing and warmth for her. "I need to get a
few things from the house. Do you want to come in?"

She shook her head adamantly, and Adam noted the
stricken, pale look of someone who had just suffered severe
shock. Whatever troubled Jillian, she couldn't speak of it
just now. She wore the ring he'd given her long ago, but
now wasn't the time to ask why. "Wait here. I should get
another horse—"

"No. Don't. I mean, please don't take time away from
what you had planned. Let's...let's just go, if it is all right
with you? Will the horse carry both of us? I could walk."

"You're not walking." Adam nodded and when he returned with extra clothing and bathing supplies for Jillian,
she was still standing where he had left her. She looked
incredibly vulnerable wearing his coat, her head bent in

thought. She barely noticed when he lifted her into the saddle and swung up behind her.

Whatever troubled Jillian would have to come out when she was ready, and Adam prepared himself for the worst. He'd made a mistake by using Sam to communicate with her, but if she had discovered that deception, she would have been angry. Right now, she acted as if she was in shock, locked in a horrible nightmare. She felt so fragile in his arms, and he eased her back against him. "It's a long ride. Sleep if you can."

"I don't think I'll ever sleep again," she whispered, relaxing slightly against him. She shook her head. "It was all so wrong."

Adam knew better than to ask questions. Jillian acted shattered and she'd need time to put her thoughts together. Waiting wouldn't be easy—but he would, for Jillian.

Eight

Adam stirred the fire and glanced at Jillian, who, like a robot, had followed his basic directions to change her clothes. She'd cared little when he'd washed her face and hands, both cold and lifeless to his touch. The incredible emptiness of her eyes tore at him. Once, just once, she'd looked at him and her expression spoke helplessness. "You'll get through this, Jillian," he said as he combed her hair. "Just take your time."

With night coming early on the mountain, she sat on his sleeping bag, dressed in his overlarge sweatsuit and draped in his jacket against the cold; his socks extended past her toes. She'd eaten little, mechanically following Adam's urging. Her arms wrapped around her knees, her chin sitting on them as she rocked, staring sightlessly into the fire.

He'd seen people stunned by war or natural disaster act the same, the mind needing the bridge to adjust from a nightmare to reality. *Jillian, Jillian*...

"Tea?" he asked, and waited for her to decide. Slowly

she reached for the cup, cradling its warmth in her hands. It grew cold as she held it, still rocking and staring into the flames. After a time, he took the cup and tossed the contents. ''How about a candy bar? You used to love them—all that gooey chocolate and nuts…''

He opened a bar and handed it to her. ''Eat.''

She stared at the candy and her voice sounded hollow, echoing whatever trauma her mind held. The first words that she'd spoken since she'd arrived at his cabin almost floated away into the night. ''You used to give these to me. You knew my parents wouldn't allow them—'Don't eat anything to spoil your complexion,' they said. I always did as I was told. I tried to please them. Everything was for Tom—he would be the one to carry on the family name. I knew just what I was supposed to do—marry well. I did. Kevin did help with my parents' bills, and he was supportive. I think we could have been friends, except for…. It just wasn't there, the feeling that should have been. I was probably the only woman not in love with him—his wife.''

Adam settled beside her on the sleeping bag. Kevin O'Malley deserved just one good punch; he would have been almost twice Jillian's weight and more in strength. Adam didn't like the anger bristling in him, nor the reason for it. ''It's a good starry night. That time was long ago, Jillian.''

''No, it's right here. Right now.'' She bit into the candy bar and chewed quickly as if determined to rebel against those rules long ago. She crushed the wrapper in her fist, tossed it into the fire and watched it ignite. ''I owe you a big apology, Adam. And my gratitude.''

Then she was on her feet, stalking across the small mountain clearing. Behind her, the horse watched curiously from amid the tall pines. On the cusp of May, the night air was cold. In summer, they would be cool and fragrant with wildflowers, the grass lush for grazing deer. Wild roses would be blooming, thorny and beautiful. Berries could be had for the picking—not the fat, cultured variety, but sweeter for the picking and the setting.

A woman who enjoyed images and color and texture, Jillian would be entranced. But now, her mind was coursing through other times, her body taut with emotions. "Jillian, come here. Your feet are getting damp."

She crossed back to him and balanced her hand on his shoulder as he tugged his boots onto her feet, tightening the laces. She searched his face as if finding something she hadn't expected. There was that tug on his hair, pulling it back from his face. She studied his features slowly, as if trying to see into him. "So here we are, you and I, after all these years."

"We're okay, you and I. We made it."

She shook her head. "No, I didn't. I watched it all unfold, the shame of my parents, the bitterness, and I was helpless. I loved them. I loved Tom."

She straightened and turned her back to him. Her body was stiff, her fists locked at her thighs as if braced to meet a painful obligation she must fulfill. She'd looked just that way—uncertain, fearful and determined—when she'd offered herself to him at sixteen. "I think...I think we could have made it, even as young as we were, if you'd taken me up on that marriage offer...if we could have moved away...if Sarah could have been well enough to come with us."

"Those are a lot of 'ifs,' Jillian. We were very young."

"You loved me, then," she said, needing the reassurance that the one perfect month they'd had was not a dream.

"I loved you then," he stated firmly. "I loved you for a long time after that."

Jillian's voice was low and uneven. "I owe you an apology for not believing you then. I just wanted everything to be like it was, that month we were sweethearts in high school, and I was dating the high school hero. They made life unbearable for you, didn't they? My parents and the rest? And it's true—Sarah was cast out from her friends—

they were too frightened for their families' jobs to defy my parents and their friends. I just found out last night from someone who knew the whole story. Maude, the court stenographer, told me everything.''

She rubbed her fingers over her temples as if to dislodge the facts. "I sat for hours, going over the dates and the articles in the newspaper archives. There was nothing there, a total lack of facts. I remembered who was connected to the judge, and the police force and the attorneys. I have no doubt that their political connections played a part, too. Oh, the records were sealed, but the facts fit. Now I'm seeing them as an adult. You paid a terrible price for keeping your honor, Adam. They literally drove you out of town.''

He shook his head. The admission must have cost Jillian, and now he knew why she was so stunned. A loyal, truthful woman, Jillian would have been devastated by the deceit. He wanted to lessen the impact, to help her. "I left because it was time for me to leave. I'd always wanted to see the world. Now I have.''

Jillian turned to him. "And there was me. I didn't believe you then. I do now. All that I can say is that back then, everything was distorted. I was so young, Adam. Sheltered from life perhaps—in some ways. But in others, I had everyday lessons in power, money and social status. Sometimes I wonder exactly what I would have been like if I would have had more loving parents. I always wanted to—never mind. Well, yes, I'll tell you. I always wanted to be just as confident as you. Maybe even now, I begrudge your traveling as you wished, not to business conferences or obligatory vacations with business friends. But really, just stretching out my hands and grasping what life offered—I've always been afraid to do that.''

"You've already done that.''

"I have?'' The thought shocked her.

"You chose your life apart from what your parents had chosen. You retrained into a field you love. You did all that.''

She shook her head. "Do you know that through everything with Kevin, I never lost my temper? I wanted to, but it just wouldn't come. It certainly comes when I'm mad at you. With you, everything has colors and meaning. I'm almost angry at you because of that—showing me the contrast between my existence and being alive, like that day you bought the pickup. It was so different from the way I've trudged through life."

He couldn't bear to see her aching. "You made something of your life, Jillian. You did it on your strength alone. Be proud of that."

Adam knew that wouldn't have helped her with Kevin; it could have made things worse. "There's nothing wrong in being safe, Jillian."

She took off the ring and handed it to him. "I threw this at you, now I'm giving it back with my thanks. As an adult, you could have tried to reopen the case, unseal the records, but you didn't. I think you were protecting me, even as I disliked you. I'm so sorry."

Adam stood and placed the ring on her finger again. He chose her left hand, smoothing the slender line between his fingers. The sight gave him pleasure, that she wore something he had given her. "Keep it for good luck. You've kept it this long—why?"

Jillian shook her head and her expression said that her heart and mind were too filled with emotions for words. Adam watched helplessly as tears began to shimmer in her eyes. "It's a whole lifetime, Adam. Yours and mine. You should have had those scholarships to go to college, but no one was feeling friendly toward you. The committee granting them had sons in that gang. So much time wasted. I tried so hard to please everyone—my parents, Kevin, and in the end, I lost myself. I— The only true happiness I've had has been here in these last months with the Tallchiefs. I'll always remember this time, holding it dear."

She looked as if she'd come through galaxies, clearly exhausted. The rigid stance was gone now, her shoulders bent. Adam couldn't bear to see her so torn. "Jillian, that was the past. You were just a girl."

"I should have— Hold me, Adam. Hold me tight," she whispered, moving close to him. There was little he could do, but hold her tight and safe against him, aching for her.

"You'll come through this, Jillian," he said against her hair. "You're a strong woman now. You've chosen your own life and you're good at what you do. You've built a career and a life—"

"A life? I functioned well in survival mode. I did what I had to do, but—" She shook her head as if she couldn't continue.

"You'll be fine. You're just tired now," Adam said, nuzzling her hair, and prayed that she would be. Clearly shattered, she was just pulling herself together to face the reality of what had happened through an adult's eyes. He couldn't bear to tell her now that the contract with Sam was all his doing.

And he had to tell her soon.

Jillian awoke slowly, luxuriously, next to Adam in the large sleeping bag. It had been borrowed from Liam, according to Michelle, who insisted on sleeping with her husband. The stars were fading now, the air cold and crisp in the predawn, and Jillian felt so light, unburdened. She'd spent a sleepless night, decided what she should do, but only the apology that had been scraped from her soul, felt right. Now forgiveness was up to Adam.

She had watched the fire for hours after Adam had tucked her into the sleeping bag, her eyes dry with crying and lack of sleep. He'd sat for a while, stroking her hair, and then she couldn't bear the thought of him sleeping with just a blanket on the cold mountain ground. "Adam, I will not be responsible for your discomfort or sickness. Either you share this with me, or I'm sleeping on that blanket."

He'd hesitated, shook his head as if he knew better, and then slowly undressed down to his boxer shorts. In the dying firelight, she'd thought how beautiful he was, how far he'd traveled, to be just here, with her, when she'd needed him.

She lay very still, feeling the different textures of a male lying next to her, Adam's heat enclosing her. He slept curled against her back, their bodies spooning, and Jillian was reminded of the feathers and the legend: *The woman who brings the hawk and the dove feathers to the hunter shall tame him in gentler ways. He will be her strength, protecting her, but she has her own powers, most tender and loving. 'Twill not be easy for the hawk and the dove, one bred to hunt, and the other of a gentler nature. Together they grow into each other's lives, and love will be born.*

Had Sarah known, so long ago, that Adam's and Jillian's lives would be twined together? They had grown into each other's lives, and now they were facing a new beginning.

He'd spoken of girl, a long time ago. *She broke my heart. I wonder at times, if it ever mended enough to let another woman into it.* Was *she* that girl? He'd seemed in love when they were in their teens—was it possible?

She turned slightly, and Adam shifted to his back. He looked so peaceful now, his breathing easy.

As if sensing she had awakened, he murmured sleepily, "Are you all right?"

"I'm fine." She wanted to touch him, to stroke his face, to feel that strength that had surrounded her last night. She trusted him—that thought ran through her as she considered how to ask him....

"What's wrong, honey?" he asked softly, turning to her. "Can't sleep?"

The endearment was deep and intimate as if he had saved it just for her. She curled the word around her, treasuring it. "These sweat clothes are warm, and you're like a furnace."

He moved as if to leave, and she placed her hand on his

bare chest, smoothing it. The textures were smooth and
powerful, the scar ripping across his arm proved that he
took his challenges and survived. She smoothed the shark
bite on his side, and images she had seen in movies terrified
her. She couldn't bear to think of Adam mangled and lifeless. "Don't leave."

He lay back, watching her in the night as she sat up and
squirmed to pull off the oversize sweatpants, then the top.
She'd never been bold, but now with Adam beside her,
watching her with that dark, flickering, hungry look, she
felt very feminine—and not at risk. *Not at risk. She felt as
if she could do anything, here on this mountain with Adam,
and it would be natural and right.*

She had to ask— "Am I the girl who broke your heart
a long time ago?"

That hard mouth changed and slid into a slight smile.
"None other. You ruined for me any other woman, sweetheart."

Her instincts told her that making love now, with Adam,
was right. She wouldn't be frightened or rigidly cold. She
wanted to be a part of him, to feel complete. She would
have no regrets, because she knew that on a primitive level,
she could trust him, if not herself. Adam would only touch
in her gentleness and in affection. She needed his warmth
and the tenderness that went with it. She also needed to
give in return. She lay down and turned to him. "Make
love with me."

The muscle in his arm brushing hers leaped as if he were
startled. He shook his head. "Jillian, you're upset. You'll
think differently in the morning. I'm not taking advantage—"

"I take responsibility for my actions. I'm not that starry-
eyed girl any longer, Adam. I'm a woman who wants you."
She bent to seal his lips with a kiss. "You're not taking
advantage. I want you. Equal opportunity, you know."

Adam studied her face, smoothed her cheek. "There's

no going back. Once I've tasted you, I'll want more. I'd rather wait until—''

"Shh. Just make love to me and everything else can wait—'' She'd never been aggressive in lovemaking, but now she moved on top of Adam. His skin burned her bare breasts, and only thin layers of cloth separated his arousal from her. She smoothed his hair away from those rugged, very warm features and traced that high cheekbone with her fingertip. "Am I making you uncomfortable?''

"No—'' Then, "Yes, very,'' he whispered raggedly as his hands slid open upon her, caressing the length of her back and lower. He glanced down at where her breasts met his chest, and a ripple shot through the powerful length of his body as he groaned unevenly. "It's not quite 'uncomfortable.' Be very certain, Jillian.''

"I am,'' she said firmly, against his lips, tasting him with her tongue. He tasted of mystery and pleasure and softness and truth, and she added, a little of edgy, wary male. The textures of stubble on his cheeks, the heat and excitement that sizzled around him, and all that long powerful body were very erotic. Boldly, she rubbed her leg the length of his rougher one, enjoying the contrast of male and female, enjoying feeling feminine and desired. "I've never been more certain in my lifetime. I feel, Adam. *I feel this is right for me, now.* I've never been impulsive, and whatever else happens, I know that I was meant to be here on this mountain with you.''

Adam rolled her over so suddenly, she caught her breath. He was big and solid and powerful, and yet he didn't frighten her. She smoothed his shoulders, enjoying the breadth and strength, the gleam of his skin in the moonlight pouring over him. He leaned over her, caught her face in his hand and lifted her chin with his thumb. "There's something I have to tell you—''

She couldn't resist moving slightly, her mouth enclosing his thumb, nibbling on the pad. Sensual play and Adam could be a very, very pleasurable activity, she decided as he tensed and sucked in his breath.

Her hand accidentally touched him, found him, and enticed by the boldness, curled around him. He trembled and she was amazed that such a light touch could bring such a volatile reaction. She skimmed her hand over his shoulder, his chest, and his tall body quivered beneath her touch. One light circling of his nipple brought a ragged intake of his breath, followed by an uneven groan.

With Adam, she felt only an aching hunger, a curiosity, not a fear. The knowledge that she was capable of sensual intimacy, and not frigid at all, excited her. She wanted everything, all of him just then. "Whatever it is, tell me later," she whispered.

With a rough growl, Adam bent to fuse his lips with hers, a hot, open, steamy kiss. She arched as his hands prowled lower, finding her intimately and delving for the warmth there. The pressure of the cloth and the tearing of it didn't frighten her as his mouth found her breasts, cruised and heated and suckled. It was not as gentle as before and yet, it was truthful. She reveled in each pleasure he gave, the deep melting warmth that came as he eased over her.

Poised above her, his arms braced to ease his weight from her, Adam hesitated as Jillian stroked her legs against his, her body aching. Each movement brought him closer, warmer, bolder....

Adam smoothed her temples with his thumbs. "This is for you to decide, sweetheart. There's no going back—I can stop when you want, but intimacy between a man and a woman isn't easily shoved back into the drawer."

She lifted her hips, easing him gently against her. The incredible sense of homecoming warmed her. "I've decided."

But Adam wasn't finished, winding a strand of her hair around his hand. "You're mine, you know. We can't walk away from this, either one of us. You took my heart a long time ago, love. You still have it. There are things to settle between us, but I want you to know that no other woman has brought me the peace you have, or the joy. Or has driven me to the edge just wanting you, thinking of you just like this in my arms. Taking you here, like this, means more than you'll know. I'll be faithful to you and I'll care for your needs as best I can.''

With the wind swaying gently in the pines and Adam's voice so deep and uneven, she knew he was pledging the best part of him to her.

''You don't bring me peace,'' she whispered. ''You bring me heat and storms and the feeling that I am free and wild and able to choose anything I want—I can be who I want and you make me feel so incredibly strong. With you, I feel so real and alive. I wish I could say 'love,' but I can't, only that I feel so close to you, almost as if the legend of the feathers were true. I choose you, Adam Tallchief. Now. Here.''

''You would be a dove, soft and warm and tender of heart, I think. Aye,'' he murmured, trembling a bit in her arms, his body taut against hers. ''Aye'' held not only agreement, but tradition, a Tallchief claiming his love.

''Aye,'' she returned as their loving began, Adam moving very slowly to complete her and waiting until she accepted him fully.

Jillian closed her eyes and let him take her to a place she'd never been, moving gently against him, easily, as if she were floating on waves and incredibly safe. She saw the feathers facing apart and then spooned together, the dove and the hawk.

The first jolt of pleasure hit her, full and hard, tossing her back, riveting her. She hadn't suspected it would come that fast—the primitive need surging out of her, driving her to lock herself to him, as the tiny explosions tore through her, enveloping her. When she was able to breathe again, to focus on Adam, who held very still above her, Jillian whispered, ''My, that was ever so nice.''

''Was it, love?'' His chuckle swept through the night and

Jillian knew she was blushing. She forced herself to not turn away, because she wasn't ashamed of her decision.

He was doing no more claiming than she, she thought boldly, the shy girl moving into womanhood, taking her due.

She wondered what would please him, and settled for a wobbly, silly smile. There was little else she could do, because her brain had stopped clear thought. Adam held still; his look was tender as he smoothed her hair from her forehead. "Still okay?"

"Marvelous." Here in the fresh, clean mountain air, she felt new and strong and very feminine. She felt as if she could reach out and touch the stars, grasp and hold them tight in her fists. She felt as if she could drive chariots across the sky, or simply smile and wonder and love.

"Mmm." He sounded so satisfied and yet when he touched her again, she knew this time would be—

The second jolt of pleasure threw her against him, her fingers digging into his arms braced at her side. Riveted by the fantastic sensations, she locked herself to Adam, keeping him. *This was how it should be,* another woman thought distantly as the waves of pleasure continued to wash over Jillian's body. *He's being very careful with you, and he wants more for you than for himself. You've never been so safe, so loved. Trust him. Release yourself, who you really are with him. Don't be afraid.*

She wanted all of him, everything, and Adam's hand slid lower, easing her hips higher as she found his throat, the pulse there, and bound him tightly within her. She heard herself cry out, and moving with Adam, felt herself struggle for release, just as he stilled, pouring into her.

What an incredible peace, she decided as Adam settled lightly upon her. His muscles quivered beneath her caress, as though the strain of holding himself away, considering her, was almost more than he could bear. She wouldn't let him go, though he moved to ease away. She wanted his racing heart against hers, feeling the beat slow with hers, his skin damp and hot against hers, male to female. The slow, gentle way he caressed her said he enjoyed touching her, being close—not in desire, but in the aftermath of loving, the demonstration of affection. When he did ease away, yet holding her closely, she wiggled her toes against his, and they moved companionably in play.

Adam kissed the side of her throat, nuzzling her. "How do you feel?"

"I don't know. I think I'm still floating, and I'm not certain I have bones, but the shooting stars behind my lids aren't there anymore."

"Mmm. They're very nice bones," he murmured, running his hand over her shoulder, then cupping and caressing her breast with his thumb. His hand moved lower and his fingers locked gently to her thigh, possessively, before they stroked and caressed and smoothed down to her knee and back up to her stomach. All the while, his lips were busy, trailing over her eyelashes, her cheeks, her ears. She could feel the pulse in him, the heat beginning again between them, and this time he came to her more hungry than the first.

She had loved his gentleness, but the slight trembling of his touch told her how desperate he was for her, just as she was for him. It was an honest touch, just as his gentle ones had been, and she knew that part of her heart was lost to his keeping.

At dawn, Jillian thought she had been dreaming, yet there was Adam, bending over her, his hands caressing, urging, heating. She turned to him eagerly, and quickly caught in the firestorm that was Adam's hunger and her own. The hawk and the dove were growing into each other's lives.

She awoke again to find Adam, dressed and sitting at the fire. Ashes rose in the smoke, like the night and the past floating away, the coals glowing. In the morning shadows.

He looked deep in thought, brooding whatever haunted him. He looked like her lover, a man who held her both gently and fiercely, even in the height of his passion.

She stretched slightly, feeling warm and safe and pleasantly satisfied. Adam's mouth had heated her body, his hands shaping her intimately, possessively, just as she had possessed him. Because he'd taken time to let her know him, she didn't fear that tall powerful body; she adored it.

"Come back to bed, Adam," she whispered softly, needing him close.

He shook his head. "We've got to talk."

"Not now." Then, because she felt too apart from him, she sat and rose from the sleeping bag, pulling the Tallchief plaid that was folded nearby around her. The air was cold, but Adam's hot look was worth the effort, taking in every inch of her body.

She'd never played the seductress, yet Adam's response excited her. She let the plaid fall away and thrilled when Adam's gaze locked hungrily to her body, her senses leaping already, needing him…. He rose and walked slowly toward her. When she reached to smooth his cheek, his hand caught her wrist, turned it to kiss her palm. Then he was easing her beneath him and she needed no covers because Adam was very warm and ready.

This time, there was no gentleness, but a fierce taking, just as she wanted. She wanted that open honesty between them, that jolting passion, the desperate hunger matching her own. Again, she heard her keening cry and knew that once more he had taken everything, and she had taken more.

He bathed her later, and Jillian had never been touched so reverently. She watched, fascinated, while he used the same soapy water in the bucket. "You look like a girl," he said, grinning at her. "I washed your clothes earlier. They should dry when the sun is a bit higher."

"I like wearing your clothes. And the Tallchief plaid. It seems right somehow that we should be here like this. I

understand a bit how Elizabeth Montclair could be so fierce
with her Liam." She inhaled the clear air, tinged with
campfire smoke, and watched a squirrel scamper up a red-
barked pine tree. Higher yet, a hawk circled lazily in the
bright blue sky, and again she called the legend: *The
woman who brings the hawk and the dove feathers to the
hunter, shall tame him in gentler ways. He will be her
strength, protecting her, but she has her own powers, most
tender and loving. 'Twill not be easy for the hawk and the
dove, one bred to hunt, and the other of a gentler nature.
Together they grow into each other's lives, and love will
be born.*

She smiled a bit to herself; the morning after lovemaking
had turned her into a true romantic. Was she in love? Probably.

Jillian straightened, caught by an image of Adam as a
small boy. She breathed very quietly, stroking the Tallchief
plaid draped around her shoulders, as she settled into her
thoughts. Unless she was mistaken, she had just experienced her first biological nesting urge. She carried the evidence of Adam's loving in her slightly aching muscles, in
the heaviness and sensitivity of her breasts and lower.

"It's not likely you'll conceive, sweetheart," Adam
noted softly. "I didn't have protection. It hasn't been a
necessity since no other woman has interested me in years.
But it's no light matter, and we'll meet it together. I should
have been prepared—I wasn't. I apologize for that, but not
for the loving. I'm old-fashioned that way it seems. I made
love to you because I care. I'll be faithful as I said, and I'll
be very careful with you. Are you feeling better?"

Underlining his responsibility, taking it, was typical of
Adam, who had stood firm in his beliefs as a boy, holding
them dear as a man. Images of a family she'd always
wanted hurled through her mind, mixed with other images
of the Tallchief children, all black hair and gray Scots eyes.
She pressed her hand low against her body and hoped—

but reality told her that the timing wasn't right for conception. "Much better. I can't tell you how sorry I am—"

Pitch ignited in the flames, hissing and throwing a flurry of sparks into the smoke. Adam's gaze narrowed at her and the air was suddenly too quiet between them. "If last night was payback for some misplaced guilt, I'm not going to be happy."

The statement slapped at her, but she understood the reasoning behind it. "I wanted to make love with you, Adam."

She studied him and decided he was ripe for her first attempt at flirtation. "I don't know why I would want you, though. You're oversize, for certain, taking up too much room in the sleeping bag."

"This wasn't a one-time-and-forgotten experience for me, Jillian," he stated firmly, and she remembered the words he'd said before they made love, as if he were taking a vow. *Taking you here, like this, means more than you'll know. I'll be faithful to you and I'll care for your needs as best I can....*

"I would call it several times, wouldn't you?" She felt marvelous, awake and ready for anything life tossed at her. She stretched and yawned and snuggled, filled with pleasure from the past night and from the lovemaking to come—

But Adam's tone was cool, as if he'd set his mind on a task. "That's just the problem. There's no going back now. We can try, but last night will always be there."

She sensed his uneasiness and she didn't want the happiness within her ruined. He'd said he had something to tell her, and whatever it was—she didn't want to know. Nothing could be worse than what had happened all those years ago. Yet she knew that Adam would have his say and a chill ran through her. "Do you have to be so solemn this morning? I can deal with whatever happens between us."

"Can you?" he asked ominously. Then, quickly he blurted, "What if I were to tell you that I'm Sam?"

Nine

"Sam? You?" Jillian smiled, mentally comparing the two men. Adam—carefree, taking life as he found it, an adventurer, unconcerned about tomorrows or business. Sam—considerate, involved in the design and production of his toys, in the uplifting morals of each story he wrote, concerned about every detail of his employees' and associates' lives, operating at a high-tech level with computers and faxes....

"*Are* you Sam?" she asked, going along with the tease and the image of Adam in a business suit.

"Yes," Adam stated firmly after a hesitation. The morning shadows deepened on the planes of his face, the angles more harsh and weary as a slash of light cruised his black blows and hit his jutting cheekbones. "I knew it wasn't right, but I wanted to know more about you—what had happened to you. You do good work, Jillian, and you needed a chance to break into larger accounts. I knew you wouldn't take an offer from me, but you might from Sam.

Saying I'm sorry isn't enough. I should have told you sooner. I tried to—''

"You *are* Sam?" she asked dully after a long moment in which her heart stopped beating. *I just made love with Sam?*

He gave her some unmistakable details that Sam would know from working with her. "I'm Sam," he said, watching her. "I was about twenty-five and driving an eighteen-wheeler. I'd pass children playing in their yards, and think, 'I'd like to give them something. I'd like to tell them to be kind to each other and to be safe by following the rules— the stop signs, the crosswalks, the railroad signs.' Sarah did the same with me. Sam was born because I needed something to fill my spare time, the hours when I wasn't working."

He shrugged lightly. "I wanted to have more money to donate for abused women and kids centers, like the one in Amen Flats, and to handicapped children. You have too much to deal with now, but I am sorry."

"Sorry." The word fell flat into the cold morning as Jillian tried to place Adam's image over the business one she had conceived of Sam. *Sorry?* she realized her voice had risen hysterically.

She hurried to grab her borrowed sweat clothes, then decided she wasn't wearing anything of Adam's; she wouldn't be obligated to him for anything more. Taking a stick in one hand, she foraged for her damp clothes on the bushes nearby while holding the sleeping bag to her chest.

While she tugged her damp clothes inside the sleeping bag and squirmed into them, Adam sat still, staring at the fire as if he expected the worst. "You can't wear those clothes, Jillian. They're still damp."

"Do not tell me what I can do!" She sat up and jammed on her shoes. "What a joke. You must be very happy with yourself, taking pity on me, giving me that fat account, making me feel important, a part of the Sam the Truck family."

He stood, towering over her. "Pity had nothing to do with it. You're good. You did a great job on the ads and now on designing the packaging. The brochure has more life than any of the other promotions."

"'Promotions?' 'Packaging?' What do they have to do with that—" She pointed to the mussed sleeping bag.

"Not a thing. That was real and if we took everything else and parceled it apart, that would still be good and true. The value is in the unseen, the intangibles—"

She stared at him blankly, full realization of his deception curling around her, squeezing her. "You're talking like Sam."

He shoved a hand through his hair. "I *am* Sam."

"Didn't you think I'd find out? What did you think would happen then?" Dazed, Jillian sat with her legs crossed on the sleeping bag and shivered, the mountain chill seeping into her damp clothes. She tossed away the coat he tried to give her.

"I thought we could make it work, Jillian. I still do."

She shook her head. "What 'work'?"

"You and me. We work well together on designs and ideas. There's no reason we can't work out our lives."

"I had one business marriage. I'm not having another relationship like that."

Adam's gray eyes narrowed and in the dim light, his mouth firmed, that jaw locking in place. "You're right in that. You're not. There's nothing cold about how you feel in my arms, Jillian. Whatever else has happened, you feel right."

"You mean sex? An affair?" The idea shocked Jillian-the-lady who had always thought she was frigid. She *definitely* had felt like a woman in Adam's arms.

"Now where would you get an idea like that?" Adam's deep voice held anger. "I intend to marry you, Jillian—"

"'Marry?' You and I? Now there's a concept that frightens me. I'd be in constant upheaval, either ready to throw something at you, or—" She didn't want to tell Adam that

there was no telling how she would act with him nearby—
for one thing, she wanted to fling herself at him now. After
all her careful planning and restructuring her life into the
peaceful zone, marrying Adam would be a disaster.

The way he made her *feel* was too shocking. And then,
there was the Sam matter. *Marriage to Adam?* A barrage
of images slammed into her and Jillian knew that she had
to sort everything out very carefully—including her family's deception.

"What are you doing?" he asked, watching her crawl
back into the sleeping bag.

It had their scent, Adam's scent, and just for a time, she
needed to remember their beautiful lovemaking—when the
world seemed to be spinning just right.

"I've had enough shocks in the past two days to last
quite the lifetime." Jillian turned her back to him and
pulled the Tallchief plaid over her. "I'm going back to
sleep. I woke up in a different world than last night. I don't
want to think anymore. When I wake up again, none of this
will have happened."

"We made love—*that* happened…. Are you going to
cry?" he asked warily, considering her.

"No. But I may shout. And if a bear comes along, tell
him I'm in the mood for a good fight. Good night."

"It's morning, honey," Adam said softly, with the sound
of laughter in his tone.

"Just go away and let me sleep."

Jillian pulled the sleeping bag over her head and closed
herself away from the beautiful morning and the discovery
that Adam was Sam. One thought held her, and she poked
her head out of the sleeping bag to find Adam staring at
her bra, very white in the morning sunlight, dangling from
a branch with her torn briefs. "Adam? You did say I did
good work, didn't you? That is the reason I was contracted,
right?"

"Very, very good. It's alive and it will appeal to my
kids."

She fumbled and struggled and finally sat up. "Your kids? *You have children?*"

Adam was very quiet. Then he stood, grabbed her bra and briefs and walked to drop them on her. "You're awake now, aren't you? Let's get off this mountain before any more damage is done. Do you really think that I wouldn't tell you something like that? I told you I was with another woman—we planned to get married. And neither one of us really wanted children. Now I do—with you, and that's the whole shocking truth, Jilly-dear. I'd like to have my own family—with you… Jillian, my wife, wearing a gold wedding band instead of that silver one and lying beside me every night."

He inhaled very raggedly as if he'd caught a thought, but it wasn't his first choice. "If I can't have you with vows, I'll take what I can get, as long as we're together."

"Now that's an image—you settling down," Jillian finally managed to say when she caught her breath. She grabbed the briefs and threw them at him, a reminder that they'd forgotten everything but each other—and that he hadn't told her everything before they made love.

"It's time. We've lost enough of it." Adam reached down to lift her up in the sleeping bag. His kiss said that he meant exactly what he'd said before he released her.

Jillian promptly sagged onto the ground, sitting with the sleeping bag around her shoulders. She'd responded to that hot, wild kiss still tearing through her and the sudden emptiness and hunger had stunned her. Adam glanced at her while he methodically packed away the camping gear and saddled the horse. Jillian teetered between safety and Adam. Her body trembled as she folded her arms across her chest. "I'm not going anywhere, Adam. I'm staying right here, until we sort this out."

"Fine. You do that." Adam walked over to her, scooped her up in the sleeping bag and deposited her on the saddle, swinging up behind her. He adjusted the bulky bag and enclosed her in his arms. "Let's just call it a day, shall we?'' he said as he began the trek down the mountain. "You're not logical now. You need time to sort things out, and you're too sexy when you're all steamed up for me not to want you. And I'm wanting you pretty badly right now. Making love wouldn't solve anything—not with the mood you're in. And I'm not going to be blamed for taking advantage of you.''

She'd always considered herself functional, intelligent and hardworking. ''Me? Sexy?''

Adam didn't answer, his expression grim. Later, when they stopped to rest the horse, Adam peeled her from the sleeping bag and put her arms into his coat as if she were a child. He lifted her back onto the horse and bent to spread and roll the sleeping bag. Then Jillian knew what she had to do— He didn't call out to her as she rode away on his horse.

It was little payback for his Sam deception and it was not typical of Jillian to react impulsively. But then, after discovering the truth about her parents ruining Sarah's and Adam's lives, Adam's lovemaking, followed by his Sam-admission, what woman wouldn't be out of character?

Jillian guided the horse through the trail used by the Tallchiefs for over a century and a half. All the expensive riding courses her parents had insisted on served her well over the rough terrain, the narrow path. She had the odd sense that she was another woman, one who had just discovered that she might not always act like a lady with the man she loved.

A hawk soared overhead, reminding Jillian yet again of the legend. What were the rules? What were the boundaries? What kind of a match would they make—she steadfast and safe and predictable, and Adam...Adam. *Adam.* He'd made love to her so gently at first, and then with just the right touch of desperation in his trembling hands, his mouth burning hers.

Well, then, Jillian decided, she'd just discovered that she wasn't always a lady with Adam Tallchief.

Suddenly, Adam stood beside the trail, the dappled sunlight spreading over his shoulders. He was breathing hard from running, his shirt torn open to expose his gleaming chest. His eyes, the color of cold steel, slashed at her as his hand shot out to capture the reins. "Having fun?" he asked.

Stunned, Jillian took in that grim, rugged look of a Tallchief male on the hunt, and knew that he could find her anywhere. Bred from a Sioux chieftain, his ability to track in the wilds was natural. Danger clung to him; he would fight for what he wanted—and he wanted her.

He considered her to be his—

Jillian mulled her anger as she shoved a strand back from her damp cheek. She was a contemporary woman with equal rights. Adam Tallchief was just as much hers. She was sweaty and angry and upset as she'd never been before, and this time, she wasn't certain that she could control herself.

She should have been frightened; she wasn't. Anger drove her now, enough to almost throw her from the saddle onto him. Jillian shivered at the thought—the primitive, unladylike image shocking her. Just as he looked now, hair caught by the wind, his eyes narrowed and that jaw contracting in anger, Adam could have leaped from the past, a man on the hunt. Jillian knew then how Elizabeth Montclair must have felt when she'd tried to run from the man she'd married.

How the English lady had felt so long ago, when she turned to meet her husband, passion for passion.

Jillian breathed unevenly—was she really a passionate woman? The answer coursed back through the pines—apparently, when it came to Adam, she was.

"It's dangerous up here. Don't ever do that again," he said as he swung up behind her and took the reins, his arms enclosing her. There was enough power and anger riding him now to hurt her, but he wouldn't. *She knew he wouldn't; on a physical level, she trusted him, but not herself.*

"I want to see proof that you really are Sam."

But Adam was silent, pulling her back tightly against him. His heart raced against her, and his breath swept roughly across her cheek, as if he'd give his soul to keep her safe.

"Satisfied?" Adam asked four hours later when Jillian turned off his laptop. She'd prowled through his work, his contacts with the company, the memos sent in reference to Nancy's development.

"Quite." She rose, nodded and walked to the cabin's door. Her head bent as though she were thinking of speaking, and then she opened the door, closing it behind her.

Adam opened it, leaned against the frame and crossed his arms as he watched her walk to her SUV.

She paused and then looked at his pickup. Where it wasn't rusted or dented, it gleamed in the morning sunlight. Jillian's gaze took in the pickup and the cabin with its wood waiting to be chopped, and boards waiting to be disposed of, and the new tires stacked on the porch, with what looked like a newer pickup hood and a better fender. She'd imagined Sam in a sleek office and wearing a three-piece suit. A crow came to rest on the top of the house, cawing at her. Adam...Sam...Adam....

Last night...this morning...lovemaking...secrets. She walked to the pickup and sat on the running board, glaring at Adam.

He should have told her sooner. Adam walked slowly to her, and she didn't move as he sat beside her. He longed to hold her, but Jillian was rocking slightly, shaking her head as she looked at the cabin.

He'd waited a lifetime for her; making love with her only sealed his fate more. "If you peel everything else away, the basic facts hold solid. I care for you," he said, tossing any pride to the wind.

She stiffened at that, but didn't look at him. Instead, her heel crushed a new stand of grass. "Sure, and that's why you maneuvered me into contract work—why we shared those endearing exchanges. Do you realize how much my life has changed in two days? Everything I believed in has been ripped out from under me. I made a fool of myself, coming here, ready to do...I don't know what, and all the time it was lies. I gave way into an impulse, a need and made love with you. Within hours, I learn I can't trust you and this time for real.''

Adam wished he could go back in time and erase his deception as Sam. ''I can only apologize. I understand now why Tallchief captured Una and Liam kidnapped Elizabeth to bring her back here. I would have done the same thing. It would have been much simpler. You'll adjust. You're logical and competent. You'll make the right decisions and you'll survive.''

''That's what I'm afraid of.''

He took her hand and she eased it away, not a good sign. She was looking at him as if he'd just flown in from another planet. He could feel her pull away from him. ''I wasn't expecting this, honey. But here it is—you and me.''

''No, we're not here.'' Jillian stood and suddenly her hand shot to his hair, holding it back from his face. She scanned his features and frowned. ''I don't know who you are, or who I am. And I'm not going to be pushed into anything. I've already been there, done that.''

''Now, sweetheart. Don't do anything rash.'' His tone warned, and the stubble of his jaw only made him look more dangerous.

Adam rose slowly, and Jillian still held his hair. ''Don't contact me. I'm finishing the contract with Sam. When I think of all the intimate things I told you—told Sam, I could just....''

Jillian blinked and remembered all the intimate things her body had told Adam. He'd opened her soul last night and she'd curled it around him; just soothing those masculine edges had given her peace.

''Let's go into town and have breakfast, honey. You'll

feel better after you've eaten,'' Adam offered conversa-
tionally, as if she weren't holding his hair in her fist. His
expression was closed and hard, those gun-smoke eyes narrowed on her face.

She released his hair, her hand warm from the sleek texture. She rubbed her palm on her thigh, and still the feel
remained. An image of his hair drifting across her skin the
night before, sensitizing her body, shook her. The raw excitement and passion she'd felt earlier when he'd tracked
her on the mountain still stunned her. Jillian-the-lady, was
also passionate. She'd have to consider the images, and
somehow make sense of them before she came apart. She'd
controlled her life, and suddenly—with Adam—she was
another woman, fierce, determined, angry, passionate, will-
ful, sensually hungry. She lived for the moment, feeding
on the fiery desire between them, when she thought her life
had settled into a comfortable, safe one.

*She wanted his baby—she wanted a part of him to carry
inside her, to love, just as she perhaps loved Adam.* She'd
given up all those dreams long ago, and they leaped to life
and she feared them. She feared herself. ''I'm going home
to a hot bath. You're not invited.''

''Well, then, take this with you,'' he said before tugging
her into his arms.

As though primed by the night of lovemaking, her body
responded instantly, her arms shooting up to lock around
his shoulders.

His fingers gripped her hair, tethering her as his lips
slanted and took hers roughly. The kiss was hard, posses-
sive and everything to ignite the woman within Jillian. She
stepped into the fire, matching him, taking, just as he took.
The greed within her sang and enveloped and flamed. They
were just a man and a woman, on a plane where only they
existed and burned and hungered.

Adam's breath was rough against her face, and Jillian-
the-lady, shocked herself by taking his hand and pressing
it against her breast, and sighing roughly with pleasure.

When the kiss was finished, she stood trying to recover her breath and Adam coolly walked away to start chopping wood. She understood immediately—Adam had left her to choose. She could walk away, or she could come to him.

He grimly, methodically raised and felled the ax. Her instincts told her to go to him, to wrap her arms around him, to take what they could both have. But the cool stare he shot her set off her temper. "It won't work!" she yelled at him.

She looked down at the foot she had just stomped. Adam was responsible for that. And for making her love him.

And for deceiving her.

And for her irrational behavior. But then, if she were a woman in love, was she supposed to be logical? Yes, she was good and angry, not a slow simmering anger, but a real thunderstorm ready to shoot lightning bolts at whoever crossed her path.

Across the distance of the sunlight and her emotions, he stood immobile, legs braced wide, one hand holding the ax, watching her. She wasn't certain how to handle the life that she had so carefully constructed, the safe life—because one look at him said he wasn't bending now—all the choices were hers.

Adam stripped off his shirt and began chopping wood again. The May sun stroked his body, every muscle and cord in beautiful harmony as he moved. Jillian stared at him, her mouth drying. She'd held that body in her arms. She'd made him a part of her, so deep and hot that she'd never forget.

Adam was right. There was no going back, not after their lovemaking. She moved in panic now, crowded by the years of fighting to find her own place in life. "It won't work," she whispered unevenly and forced herself to drive away.

With Adam, she'd jumped from fear of a man's touch to the hunger for it. Desire, that feeling of her soul touching his as they made love, had changed her. Who was she?

How could she feel so primitive, so bold and wanton in his arms? How could she become the taker?

When Jillian made her move, he'd make his, Adam decided a month later. The last of May was in full bloom, a spray of pioneer roses beginning to climb up the old cabin.

He hadn't been able to give the launch of Nancy his full attention, distracted by memories of Jillian sighing sweetly against him. He worked on his truck, sanding and replacing and welding and tuning, but Jillian never left his mind. He thought of her sitting in it, delighted by her tractor drive, hugging the box of jars to her as if they were precious....

He glanced at the duffel bag he had packed a week ago; after a solid month of hanging on every word about Jillian, dreaming about her, he'd reached the breaking point. In the past, if a situation didn't suit him, he wasn't involved, but now he was, heart and soul. Jillian had finalized her contract with Sam the Truck and she wasn't taking e-mail from the company. She wasn't visiting the Tallchiefs.

"She's holed up," Adam murmured, and knew that he couldn't wait much longer to see her, to talk with her, to hold her. Whatever Jillian was going through, she didn't want any reminder of him. The complimentary sets of Nancy were refused at the post office.

She might well be carrying a reminder of their night on the mountain, and that thought, that hope bound him heart and soul.

Adam's smile mocked himself. No doubt his ancestors sought to possess women by giving them children; or perhaps the biological need was there, lying in him all these years. The image of Jillian, holding his baby, sent a sharp tear of emotion through his heart. Those dreams from so long ago curled around him, but Jillian was a strong woman, sorting out her life, and she would have her own dreams and needs.

He could only hope that she didn't hate him.

He looked out of the cabin window to the sunset spreading over the framework of Liam and Michelle's new home. Working full-time on the house wasn't enough to drain away the need to see Jillian. Or the need to hold her.

She'd made trips from town, but she always returned to that little cottage. Maybe it was her fortress, her safe place from the world.

What was she doing now, snuggling in that old bed beneath the quilt? Adam slapped his open hand against the wall, and pushed down the impulse to go to her. He hadn't realized how instinctive the need to capture a woman was, until he'd listened to Liam speak of courting Michelle—"She held everything of me, all that I was, all that I wanted to be, right in her hand."

Brooding, Adam slashed his hand across the stubble on his jaw. He could still feel Jillian move against him, still taste her, hear her voice, and she haunted every minute of his days and nights. He couldn't leave and he couldn't stay, not when he knew that the sight of her would cause him to go after her. It was no easy task for a hunter to stop hunting what he desired more than anything in his life.

He should leave, give her more time to think, but couldn't, moored by the chance that he might see her again.

Jillian had years to unravel, and Adam had just discovered that he lacked patience when dealing with her. He glanced at the bag of wool, his share of the Tallchief shearing, and thought of Jillian weaving and spinning at Elspeth's house, the serenity in her expression, the graceful movements of her hands and body.

A month was long enough, Adam decided abruptly, and reached for the bag of wool. Within minutes, he parked the pickup outside her cottage, hefted the bag of wool and carried it up her steps to her porch. He rapped on the door.

She opened the door and his first sight of her squeezed his heart—she'd been crying and looked all soft and warm and cuddly. The scents of her bath and shampoo curled around him, the towel still wrapped upon her head, her bathrobe tied at her waist. He wanted to hold her—instead he said flatly, "Wool. My share. It's been cleaned and carded—I helped Elspeth. Make something…or don't. I bought the farm from the people who sold me the pickup. I've never owned a home before, never wanted to. I may move into it—or not. I haven't decided— I miss you. The spinning wheel comes with it, a big old scarred thing that seems to hum when it turns."

He mentally mocked himself for not being able to tell her more—how he wanted to hold her now. He couldn't bear to watch her struggle for composure, to bring up her shields, not against him.

Then she ripped the towel from her head and tossed it aside, her eyes lashing at him. Whatever was locked behind that firmed mouth wasn't sweet from her expression. He turned and walked away, his belly still tight with tension as he drove to Liam and Michelle's house to baby-sit J.T. Later, at his cabin, he stopped himself from calling Jillian. Time, he thought, she needs time to sort what's important.

The next night, he found himself at her doorstep again. She had that unfocused look, as though she'd been working on the computer and the images still held her. Her hair was loosely knotted on top of her head, the short, flowered cotton shift making her seem more like Jilly-the-teenager, than a woman he'd made love to on Tallchief Mountain. He slipped Sarah's locket into her hand, adding a kiss to it. In the locket was a picture of his mother and himself, the gold flower design worn smooth by age.

"It's true, what my brother says, that a man's love can hold his heart in her hand," he murmured, watching her face, the way the shadows skimmed across it. Jillian frowned and opened her hand, the gold chain sliding between her fingers, the silver ring gleaming just where he had placed it. Then she slowly closed the door. Adam stood still, praying she would invite him in, but the lights suddenly clicked off.

Waiting for one word, one look wasn't easy. Staying was more difficult, but Adam braced himself again the next night. He handed her the wildflower bouquet he'd picked, mixed with heather from Tallchief Mountain. While he was waiting for just one word, she narrowed those amber eyes and bashed him with the bouquet, then shut the door.

"Progress," he murmured tightly, and hoped her reaction truly was. Not sweet, but then what ran between them was more potent than he had expected.

By the first week of June, he was short-tempered, chafed raw by lack of sleep and not happy about his solitary life. He was ready to confront Jillian and give her what was left of his pride. In the grocery store, buying his supply of suckers for the children he baby-sat, the hair on the back of his neck lifted. Adam turned slowly to the fruit section, where he found Jillian scowling at him. He nodded and smiled.

"Marry me and I'll make you a loom to go with that spinning wheel," he offered, because the thought had long been on his mind, and he could use the pattern of Una's pioneer loom.

The woman checking out his groceries was a grandmother who looked younger than her years. Adam ignored her smothered giggle, and caught the orange that Jillian had fireballed his way. He placed it on the counter. "That, too, please."

After several oranges, the clerk began to sack them. "She's headed toward the grapefruit. You must have really goofed. You Tallchief boys really know how to stir up your lady loves. She was a lady when she came here, now she's pitching fruit at you."

"Ah, thank you, Millie. 'Lady love' is just the right term. Do you hear that, Jillian? You're my lady love. Hey, you're good—" He caught the grapefruit that sailed his way, and the clerk happily bagged them. "When do I start on the loom, dear heart?" he asked lightly.

"Not the melons, honey," the clerk called firmly as Jillian moved slightly in the produce aisle. "Avocados will do."

"Avocados are too good for him," Jillian noted, quickly walking past Adam on her way to the door. After glancing at the sucker he offered her with a smile, she shook her head. She smoothed her hair and straightened her blouse and sailed out of the store with her head held high.

"Try something a little more romantic next time," Millie offered. "And if she's not in a better mood by the time tomatoes are ripe, don't come in here."

Adam tilted his head to better watch the enticing sway of Jillian's jeans and forgot what he was thinking.

"Give her time," the clerk said. "Everyone knows a girl can't resist you Tallchief boys when you're in the courting mood."

"Oh, she knows how to resist," Adam said broodily and picked up the sacks he intended to leave on Jillian's doorstep that night.

But that night, when she opened the door, Adam pushed it wider—his earlier burning conversation with Liam included her. She'd confronted Liam and told him that she knew Sarah, and she wouldn't have anyone thinking ill of her. At first, Liam hadn't responded and then he'd told her to mind her own business. Jillian hadn't backed down, and Liam had promptly called Adam. "I know how you feel about Sarah. That's good enough. Just don't ask me to share those feelings. And call off Jillian. Once that woman gets her mind locked on bull-dogging a man into something, she doesn't let go."

Adam placed the sacks of fruit just inside the door. He glanced at her sleeveless print blouse and her jeans, those slender bare feet that had played with his in the sleeping bag. No matter how plain the clothes, Jillian always looked as if she were a lady.

Too bad, he thought, determined to have his say. He forced his gaze from her toes and his mind from her body, close and soft and bare, against his. "I don't need you interfering between Liam and myself. You had quite the chat with him earlier in the day, didn't you?"

She lifted her chin, then as he had done, slowly took in his black T-shirt and jeans and comfortable moccasins. "Someone had to do something. You two are moving around each other, working together on their new house, but you're not communicating about the wall between you—Sarah. She wouldn't have liked that, Adam. She's a big part of your life."

"Liam and I are getting along fine."

"No, you're not. You're both circling the issue. He's bitter about Sarah's deceit and you aren't trying to understand that. He's not trying to understand how you feel. I merely showed him Sarah's locket with the picture of you and your mother inside. If Sarah could have, she'd have taken both of you to raise. She was a loving woman."

"We were brought up differently. We're going to think differently. He said you told him that unless we settled this, the gap between us would widen, and you would be forced to take action. Exactly what action, Jillian?"

"I'll think of something. Michelle will help me. You've had Sarah's softness in your life, use it now with Liam." Jillian pointed in the direction of Liam and Michelle's house and then placed her hands on her waist. "He's your brother. You go over there right now, and you listen to what he has to say. You tell him about how Sarah treated you, and the good things you remember. His own childhood was terrible, and you should give him the best of yours. You haven't said a word about Sarah, avoiding her name, because you don't want to hurt his feelings. Just do it, Adam. Now."

Adam stood very still, the sweet night air curling around him, mixed with Jillian's scent. No one had ordered him to mend emotional fences in his lifetime. Before coming to Amen Flats, if a situation got too tense or emotional, he simply moved on. While he was circling the order she'd just given him, he asked, "When you go out of town, is it because you can't stand staying here? Are you leaving? Do you want *me* to leave?"

Are you carrying my baby? he wanted to ask. But the decision to tell him was hers.

"I wouldn't think of it. I'm not done with you yet. By the way, I was just absolutely aghast at the way I behaved in the grocery store. You bring the most primitive feelings out in me. I haven't decided quite what to do about it. If you leave, that's your choice. But I'm staying. I am not budging until I unravel what you've done to me."

"What *I've* done to you?" Once more the fever between them that night danced around Adam. "Did I hurt you? I tried—"

"I actually nibbled on you, Adam. I behaved unlike myself. I lost control for the first time in my life. Controlling my needs and life is very important to me."

She took a deep breath, as if bracing herself, and looked out into the June night. "I went to see Kevin. He's never going to be quite successful in politics, but he'll hold minor offices. His parents had done all the running for him, but they've gone as far as they can. Whatever he does from now on will have to be on his own merit. I'm not taking the blame for his failure. He said that our divorce had ruined his career, and...I...hit him. He was trying to browbeat me again, calling me 'frigid' and since now I know that I am not—I hit him, right in the stomach. Just that little violence felt rather good. It was closure. And then I thanked him for all that he had done for my parents to make them more comfortable—it was only the right thing to do."

"Did he hurt you?" Adam thought of how Kevin could have—

"Of course not. He was too shocked. I've always been very proper. And then I visited Sarah's grave and had a refreshing chat with her. Then, a few more chats with some of Tom's friends, in which they clarified what a real bully he was. When they feel up to it, they're coming here and they will apologize to you. After that, I came home and made jam and started working on new projects."

"You did *what?*" No one had interfered in his adult life, and he wasn't having her try to right old wrongs for him.

"I made jam and started working on new projects," she repeated, then more softly, "They are just men now, Adam, with their own children, and guilt isn't an easy burden to bear. Closure is so important. You'll listen and you'll talk with them."

Adam shoved his hand through his hair. He didn't like the uncertainty Jillian could bring him, and dealing with the past was too painful. "*I* should let *them* ease their consciences? Give *them* closure? Why?"

"Because you always do what is right. They were young and impressionable and frightened, just as I was. You were stronger than all of us, and you still are. They've never forgiven themselves. There were tears in their eyes when we talked, and it was all so wrong. All of us need to adjust to the past somehow, to live with the same pride and honor as you have. They owe you apologies, and it was important to me that someone—me—did something, though too late, to help you now."

She left the doorway and returned with a jar, handing it to him. "Strawberry. Good night."

He stared at the jar, running his finger over the old raised trademark. "I don't need you fighting my battles, Jillian."

"I know. I should have helped a long time ago, and all that I did was to hold Sarah's hand as she slipped away. It wasn't enough. It isn't enough now. I owed it to her and to you. Good night."

Adam stood facing the closed door and holding the jar of jam. He frowned; uncertainty hadn't been a part of his life, nor was sorting out painful emotions he'd kept locked too long. He knocked on her door again, and when Jillian opened it, he asked, "I'm not making any promises. My brother is the only one who concerns me. What am I supposed to say?"

"You'll think of something. Oh, you look so stunned. I know, you haven't had to work on relationships before, at

least not at close range. And it will be good for you, too.
I suspect you've never truly grieved. As Sam, you would
have named a truck after her, but you didn't. Here, take
this with you—'' She stood on tiptoe and kissed his cheek.

When the door was closed again, Adam shook his head
and placed his free hand over her kiss. It had shaken him
more than any wharf bully's fist. Life wasn't so bad when
a man had a kiss in one hand and a jar of jam from his
lady love in the other, he decided, inhaling the fragrant June
night. He sat on the porch's old oak chair, the jam on his
knee, and wondered about the caring kiss she'd given him.

Liam drove by; he reversed and stopped in front of Jillian's house. Adam held up the jar of jam like a trophy,
and Liam came to sit on the steps. Jillian came out of the
house, glanced at Adam, and handed Liam a jar of jam
with the stern order, ''Talk and listen.''

When she moved to sit in the chair next to Adam, he
placed the jam on the floor and tugged her into his lap. He
hadn't needed anyone in his adult lifetime, and now he
desperately needed Jillian. ''Stay.''

Struggling to survive, he'd never fully grieved for Sarah,
and with Jillian on his lap, smoothing his hair, the love he
felt for Sarah came more easily into the night.

Old and sweet, the memories came back to him and he
gave them to Liam—how Sarah packed them into a car to
go camping, because the other boys were camping with
their fathers. ''She didn't know how, but she had studied
manuals and books for weeks. She was like that, giving me
everything no matter the cost to her. She was always right
there, in the front row of the audience at any of my school
activities. I knew she would always listen.''

Once started, Adam's Sarah-stories came easily, as if
they had been waiting to be released and shared with Liam.
Adam gave them carefully, one by one, the treasures of his
heart, and ended slowly saying, ''We always had chocolate
cake for special occasions because she knew it was my
favorite. And that's how she was—loving and giving.''

When his throat tightened, Jillian leaned her head against his and smoothed his cheek. "I know, Adam. You loved her very much and you were so hurt by the cruelties to her. But she's in you, right there in your heart."

Adam held her hand over his heart, unable to speak. He felt as if a tight knot inside him had just unfurled. Liam stood slowly and spoke quietly. "It must have been very hard for you, and for her. I can understand better why she wanted to insure that some part of our parents stayed with her, a part of her sister and the man she loved all that time. You're right, she should be remembered well. I'll try to think of her without the anger now—because she loved you."

When he'd gone, Adam sighed and placed his face against Jillian's throat, needing her softness and comfort. Later, he might return to withholding his emotions, but just now he needed her. The light caress of her hand on his hair soothed the remaining pain inside him now. "I've never told anyone those stories, or how I felt. I didn't realize until tonight how much of it has been locked in me—I'd better go."

"Oh, no, you're not," she whispered, then her lips were against his, sweet and soft and enticing. Adam could do little but lift her in his arms and carry her inside.

Ten

"Jillian…" In her house, Adam slowly eased her to her feet, fearing that in his need, he would touch her too roughly. The need to hold her close and make love with her was more than sexual, it was to bond his life with his love's.

"Adam…"

She framed his face with her hands, and Adam held very still as her light kisses circled his face, his brow, his eyelids, his cheeks. His hands rested on that slight waist, lightly, so lightly, as he held back his impulse to hold her tight. His restraint served him well; the magic of her touch healed and softened and shared. With her arms around his waist, she rested her head on his shoulder, and Adam held his breath with the tenderness enveloping him. Turning her lips to his throat, Jillian nuzzled against him as though she were coming home.

He swallowed heavily, bound by tender new emotions,

fearing to speak, taking every touch, every caress into him to hoard.

When Jillian eased away, Adam knew it was her right to choose. He stood still, aching for her, unable to move, to speak. She circled the room, locked the door, turned off the lights and walked slowly into the small bedroom and began undressing in the dim light. Her body swayed, the movements graceful as she folded back the old quilt, and slid between the sheets.

"Come to bed, Adam," she whispered as he stood, locked in place, unable to move.

He moved to the bedroom doorway, bound by the sight of Jillian's hair spread across the white pillowcase, the curve of her body beneath the sheets. "If this is because—"

"This is for me, Adam. I need to know if what happened between us was real…if you really held me so tenderly, became a part of me, so deeply that I'll never forget."

"I want you," he said, and realized how blunt and ragged the words sounded, echoing in the feminine bedroom.

"Come to me, Adam," she repeated softly.

He undressed slowly, methodically, folding his clothes and placing them on a small fragile chair. He paused by her dresser, the strand of her grandmother's pearls running beneath a picture of them at the high school prom. The beaded headband blended with the pearls as if Jillian had been holding them both, thinking of what they meant to her.

She lifted the sheet as he lay down beside her, her breast warm and soft against his arm. He intended for her to set the mood, but just that touch turned him to her, bending over her. He smoothed back her hair and wondered how she could look so serene and so warm and inviting at the same time.

Her hand caressed his face, while the other moved slowly upon his chest, his back. "Oh, it happened all right," she

whispered while he tried to restrain his hunger, his hand
already at her breast, treasuring it.

One touch, a gentle sweep over her body and lower, that
soft cry and arch of her body told him that he was not
alone in his driving need to be one with her. Suddenly,
Jillian tensed and placed her hands on his chest, easing him
away and to his back. She moved over him, and Adam
thought he would never forget the sight, the intensity of
her face, the warm pulse enclosing him.

She began to move more quickly and Adam forgot his
good intentions, his mouth seeking hers, his hands on her
hips, the flow of her body against his, taking and giving
and tightening—

Her cry, that gentle constriction set off his own and
Adam lost control, flying with her into that hot, pulsing
starburst. He held her close, fearing that she was only the
dream, not the woman. Jillian rested over him, her legs
tangled with his, her uneven breath cruising across his
throat, her body trembling in the aftershocks of their passion.

He rested with her, dazzled by the sensations, the scents,
the heat of her body. He smoothed that sleek hair back from
her damp cheek and found that soft, warm mouth, treasuring the taste and the lingering pleasure of holding her.
Then Jillian was kissing him, seeking him again, her body
restless and flowing against his, and Adam forgot everything but loving her.

Turning her suddenly, surging into her, Adam tried to be
gentle and slow. Deep in the pounding pulse, wrapped in
her scents, her arms and legs, her body flowing against his,
Adam fought the desperation to take her too quickly. The
need was primitive, arising sharply to claim her.

But her teeth nipped his shoulder, his ear, setting him
off, and the jolt shot through him like electricity. Jillian
arched, taking him deeper and Adam flew with her, his kiss
perhaps too savage, but met by her own hunger. He reveled

in her sounds, the pleasured deep purrs that spoke of hunger and need and the intensity of their lovemaking.

He shifted slightly, stroking that long slender thigh and enjoying the quiver of soft hot flesh, the ragged groan erupting from her, those dark sultry eyes watching him. She panted softly, as they paused in the pleasure, storing it, anticipating what would come.

No words were needed as Adam bent to cherish her breast, taking it in his lips, biting gently, suckling, before moving to the other. Jillian held very still, her hands holding him to her, her body lifting and leaping to his pleasure. "Take me now," she whispered with just the desperate tone that matched his own.

They were one, coming together, fighting for the ultimate release, no gentle emotion, but the truth between them. Bound by heat and the tempest and need, they crested, gave and took and slowly eased.

When Adam could lift his head, Jillian stared blankly at him, her heart racing beneath his hand. She smoothed his cheek and smiled slowly, gently, sleepily. "Don't leave me, Adam," she whispered as she drifted into a deep sleep, curled next to him.

Adam dozed and at the first light, eased from Jillian's bed. She turned to him sleepily, then as though realizing what had passed, her eyes widened as Adam pulled the blanket over her bare breasts. In the predawn shadows, her blush was beautiful, her eyes easing from his. "Stop grinning. I know exactly what I did. You caused it, Adam Tallchief."

"Well, so I did. Equal opportunity, isn't that what you wanted?"

"I was...ravenous. Not ladylike at all. What you must think of me—"

Adam couldn't resist sweeping away the quilt and bending to kiss her breasts.

"I can't think when you do that," she whispered unsteadily.

"Keep that in mind," he said as he began dressing. "I don't want the whole town talking about my pickup parked in front of your house all night."

He ducked the pillow she threw at him, and the sight of her sitting up, holding her knees, almost pulled him back to her. The memory would keep his body humming and hungry all day.

Jillian hadn't hunted a lover before, and unable to concentrate later that day, she found Adam at the Tallchief Cattle Ranch. She saw him easing down on a horse that hadn't been fully broken, and terror held her immobile. The horse hit the side of the corral, spun and kicked, and still Adam held tight, his expression grim and determined.

Her hands rested over her wildly pounding heart, her throat dry as he swung down from the horse and walked to talk to Duncan. Then Adam saw her, and the hard lock of his eyes riveted her. That stark expression said that he was a part of her and she was a part of him, and that he would be coming for her. His gaze moved slowly, possessively, down her body as if he wanted her then. As if he could carry her off, or if the scene were private, have her where he caught her. Adam didn't look away when Duncan spoke, but started to walk toward her.

The fierce hot need shot at her through the distance, Adam's gray eyes unwavering. The sunlight gleamed almost blue-black on his hair, the wind catching it. The planes and angles of his face were that of a man now, more muscle in the throat and in the breadth of his shoulders, but still those narrow hips, those long legs. In a faded cotton shirt and worn jeans with a tear at the thigh, he was just perfect for a woman to tend. Or take. Striding in the sunlight, he was magnificent, strong, the confident, conquering male, taking away her breath. She blended the image with another one, the boy, carrying his football helmet after a winning game, walking toward her.

There was just that bit of swagger, of arrogance to challenge her now, to test her as a woman, to excite her in a different way.

Standing in front of her, he hooked his thumbs in his belt and tilted his head, studying her. She'd never blushed before Adam and the warm upward sweep of color startled her. She felt exposed, hot, rosy and—very, very ripe for loving. "I'm new at this," she managed. "Please don't ever ride like that again."

"I'm new at it, too. I missed you and the horse seemed like a good distraction. Otherwise I would have come back and—" He tugged her into his arms, and Jillian stood on tiptoe to meet his kiss, her hands tethering that wild black shaggy mane she loved.

"Let's take a ride," he said abruptly, and lifted her in his arms. He carried her to his pickup and tugged her close to him as he drove.

When he stopped in a secluded cove of pine trees, he turned to her. Jillian trembled, anticipating what would come, eager for his body, to have him hold her in that sweet, hungry way. Adam's smoky eyes warmed as they took in her body, ready for him.

"Jillian," he whispered unevenly, and now just the warmth of color darkened his cheeks. Just as she wanted, he scooped her close to him, his lips already upon hers, his hands busy with their clothing. A strap of her bra tore free, and as Jillian pulled on his shirt, wanting him against her, his buttonhole tore.

He trembled when he came to her, and just there was the reverence in his touch, that slight pause that told her that he tempered his strength, fearing to hurt her.

Then the tempest began, body against body, heat and hunger mixed. Desperate for him, Jillian framed his jaw with her hands, locking that beautiful, exciting mouth to hers as Adam made love with her, moving as one.

When Jillian surfaced, she lay beneath Adam, a bird peering through the windshield at them. She'd never been so content, smoothing Adam's shoulders, his back, drifting in the sweet lingering of his breath and slow kisses against her throat. His lips curved against her skin. "This pickup seat is too short and I think I got a bruise or two from the gearshift. Are you all right?"

She stretched luxuriously. "Better than all right. I'm perfect. Show me your bruises and I'll kiss them."

Adam lifted his head to look down at her. "Don't start anything we can't finish. I'm supposed to ask you to have dinner at Duncan's."

She tried to rise and Adam gently pushed her down on the seat. "Adam, I've got to go home and change."

That dark smoky gaze lingered on her face, touched her swollen lips, and eased down the length of her body, a bra strap caught on her shoulder, the blouse still on one arm. "You look fine to me and there's no time."

"I can't go—"

"Sure, you can," Adam said as he pulled her upright and started to dress her. From the dashboard, he took a safety pin and fastened the torn strap to her bra, bending to kiss her there and to find her sensitive nipples beneath the lace. She held her breath as another aftershock of their lovemaking hit her.

"You'll come then?" he asked, carefully fastening another safety pin beneath her blouse where the button was missing.

She looked down at her wrinkled cotton print blouse, her wrinkled slacks, and gave the only answer she could. "Love to."

When they stood in front of the old Tallchief homestead, the entire family was relaxing on the front porch, children running across the yard, playing tag. Another Jillian would have been perfectly groomed, calm and controlled, socially adept at meeting any situation. Images of how she had looked at other family gatherings—dressed expensively, wearing heels and pearls and gold, and a stiff, false smile came to her mind. Instead of a limousine parked in the driveway, she'd ridden in an old truck, snuggled close to

Adam, teasing him with kisses as he drove. With the Tall-chiefs, she wouldn't need to make meaningless conversation or to conceal her bruised heart with a smile.

As she stood in the sunlight, Jillian's legs were weak from lovemaking, her body sated and heavy, and she felt wonderful. The best she could manage as she stood there in wrinkled clothes, safety pins and her blush, was an uncertain smile.

Adam put his arm around her waist and tugged her close, protectively. She glanced at him for reassurance, noted his torn buttonhole and the narrowed, steely look he gave the Tallchiefs. Though they wouldn't remark on the lovers' appearances, Adam's expression, the tense lock of his body, said that she was his; that he would fight to keep her.

The afternoon flew by, with Adam holding her hand, with her feeding him a tidbit. The gestures were small, but thrilling and Adam's deep rumbling laughter stunned her. Once while he was lying on the floor, playing with Sam the Truck, she passed and he reached out to circle her ankle with his hand. The long, lazy, smoldering look he gave her, said that he was thinking of making love.

He caught her in the kitchen, eased her into a dark closet, and kissed her again, just as hungrily, his hands moving over her, caressing and heating. When they emerged, Jillian couldn't think about anything but Adam. She smoothed her hair and her clothes as she leaned against the wall for strength. "I'm not certain this is normal for people our age," she managed to say huskily, her lips sensitive from his kisses. "I think I'm going home now. It's been quite a day."

"We've got some catching up to do. I can't keep my hands off you, and I'm starting to wonder if I ever will." Adam's hands rested on the wall beside her head; his gaze lingered on the lips she had just licked with her tongue. He toyed with a strand of her hair. "Come see me tonight at the bar. I'm working."

She almost said that she hadn't ever been to a tavern,

but in the end, with Adam looking down at her, she nodded. "I'd be happy to. What's the appropriate dress?"

He chuckled at that. "I'd rather you didn't wear anything at all and that we were alone."

At noon the next day, Jillian gripped another jar of jam and walked toward the old farmhouse. Her body ached, from the night's loving and from the anticipated confrontation with Adam. The day was bright and blue and perfect with spring sunshine—perfect for her mission.

Country taverns weren't so bad, not when you're wearing pearls and a nice sweater and slacks set—and Adam was holding her as they danced. He'd held her much tighter at her house, their lovemaking sweet and long, each touch more lovely than the previous.

Adam had slipped away before dawn. Sated and exhausted, Jillian had barely felt his kiss. She'd awakened late, lying amid the tangle of sheets. She'd nuzzled his pillow and tugged it close against her, aching for Adam. She'd taken her time, drawing her bath and sipping her morning tea while resting in the soothing herbal scents. Jillian wondered what to do with a man who would leave her alone in the morning-after.

She shook her head and glanced at the milk cows in the pasture, the rusty old tractor and Adam's battered pickup truck. The two-story, white farmhouse needed tending, the former elderly residents unable to meet its needs. The barn was in worse shape, the sheds and outbuildings slanted with age.

Yet it was a dear old place, with pioneer roses dancing along the old fence, and patches of other flowers starting to color.

Suddenly the ram that had terrorized her that day rounded the corner of the porch, staring at Jillian. "You're not keeping me from him, you know. So you and I might as well be friends."

He eyed her warily, much as Adam had done, and on

instinct—because now she seemed to move more on womanly instincts than those of reserve that she had been taught—Jillian stretched out her hand.

The ram shook his head and snorted, but he came slowly to her hand, angling his head for more petting and scratching. As if he'd gotten his desserts, he snorted once more and trotted off to his flock.

The old rooster perched on the aged porch swing didn't look friendly. He stretched out his burnished red wings and shook his black head, the red comb waggling a threat. "Shoo, now. I'm certain that we'll get along, but I've no time to spare with you right now."

One more male blocked her path, a big gray tomcat who rolled in front of the door, his belly up and waiting for a petting. She bent to scratch and pet and he allowed her to gently push him aside as she opened the ancient screen door.

Bald and barren in the bright daylight, the floors inside were old hardwood, needing refinishing; dull spots showed where furniture had rested and bright patches where pictures had hung on the wallpaper. The house had warm echoes of parents cuddling children, of a man and a woman talking quietly as they decided life moments, of meals served around the family table, of the peace that came when children slept, of the excitement when they awoke.

An old spinning wheel stood framed in the sunlight square of the window and was draped by the Tallchief plaid.

Drawn by it, Jillian walked to smooth the plaid, smiling a bit as she thought of how Adam looked that first morning, dressed in a kilt and the plaid and sweeping into her quiet home. He slashed apart what was left of the peace she'd made in life. He'd taken away the fear that plagued her, that of not being a woman who could love and respond to a man.

He'd given her more, and now she was here to take the rest.

He stepped out of the shadows, just as bold as that morning when they'd met again.

"Why have you come?" he asked bluntly, and Jillian understood that raw question covered the deep emotions inside him.

"Why did you leave me this morning?" she returned, gripping the soft wool for an anchor for her trembling hand.

He moved closer, his footsteps muted by the moccasins, his hands in his jeans' back pocket, the white T-shirt stretched across his chest. He'd been unhappy with her meddling in his life and the apologies he would hear, and the memories they would bring nagged at him now. He still ached for Sarah, for the pain she suffered and how helpless he'd been at the time. Adam wanted no part of his computer and business now, no telephones to disturb him, no brother's new home nearby. He'd come here to brood, and to question his right to the Tallchiefs—and to her.

Jillian braced herself for what she must do, and handed him the jar of jam. "I meant to tell you last night that there will be no baby. You waylaid me, as you often do, but you should know. I understand better now how difficult it was for you to find the right moment to tell me about Sam."

He studied the jam, his thumb rubbing the stamped insignia. "A jar of jam and no baby," he said hollowly. "I used prevention after that first time, but I had hopes…if that was what you wanted, too."

She brought the plaid to her face, rubbing it on her cheek. One spin of the wheel beside her brought a ticking noise, softer than the beating of her loud heartbeat. "I wanted you to know that you're not obligated—"

His hand slashed out, stopping her. "'Obligated?' Is that what a child of mine would bring you? An obligation?"

Jillian braced herself; clearly dealing with Adam would always be emotional. "I wanted you to know that you're free to go, or to stay. But if you share my bed again, you're not leaving it as you did this morning."

"Rules, Jillian? Telling me what to do?" Adam placed

the jar on an old table, and crossed his arms over his chest. Unshaven, his eyes shadowed and his jaw set, he could look formidable. But she knew that his emotions tangled inside him, the uncertainty that what they shared could hold true in bad weather, the fear that he wouldn't be all she would need. She knew, because those fears were her own. She refused to back away, to shield what ran inside her—the need to be with Adam all the rest of her life; they'd wasted enough time, rather others had wasted it for them. Now, no one else could sort their loves. "Don't try that dark, dangerous-gunslinger look with me. I won't have you—''

"Do you think I want the town talking about you? Do you think I want to sneak around, taking what I can? Do you think I want to make love to you and to wonder each time if you are giving it because we both loved Sarah and we're mending our loss?''

She reached to spin the old wheel again, still Sarah ran on his mind, *click-click, spin-spin.* Time and love would ease that pain. "We *both* loved Sarah. But she's not here now—just you and me. And we have decisions to make. I'm staying in Amen Flats. I have a home here, and a business I love. I am not taking large accounts, they're too draining, and I'm wanting more of life—I've lost so much. But I think I can fashion a nice little income from what I learned as a sales executive, and what I can bring in as a graphic artist. I want to fill out the corners of my life, the emptiness of the past years. You're right, Adam. We can't go back. We can only go forward.''

He reached to smooth her hair, then his hand eased away. "I'm an impatient man, honey—not used to waiting. Tell me why you came.''

She reached out to grip his T-shirt and Adam looked at her warily. "If you run out on me this time, Adam, I'm coming after you,'' she stated. "I'll hunt you down and bag you.''

That brought the grin she loved, all devastating male—fascinating and adorable. "You'll have to marry me to keep

me and the spinning wheel and the loom I'll build you,"
he said, with just that arrogant tilt to his head.

She couldn't resist gently teasing him and wondered
again how much laughter and life she had missed without
Adam. "Oh, I intend to. It's a lovely spinning wheel. I
couldn't bear to let it slip away. Or the loom."

The grin slid into a slight frown. "Jillian, I've traveled
nearly all my life. I don't have much to give you."

"You'll think of something. You've already given me
back myself," she whispered, loving him. "I love you,
Adam. I always have."

He considered her so intensely that Jillian braced herself
for what he might say. Suddenly shy of him and how he
was looking at her, she eased away, glancing at the old
stairs leading upstairs, and into the kitchen, the large pantry
lined with empty jars that needed filling. "This is a lovely
home, Adam—oh!"

He'd spun her around, lifting her off her feet, holding
her, his face level with her own. The expression in his face
said more than words, and she framed his face with her
hands, slanting her lips for a soft kiss.

Adam hitched her higher, his hands cupping her bottom
as she wrapped her legs around him. It seemed only right
to wrap the plaid around Adam's broad shoulders, the
length enclosing them both. The kiss changed and fused
and ignited, and soon Adam lowered her to her feet, his
hands busy with her clothes and his, and her hands flew to
touch him as she could, eager to be one with him.

With the soft breeze flowing through the open upstairs
window, the air fragrant with flowers and earth and new
life, Jillian lay spent and happy on an old soft quilt with
Adam. The world outside drifted in its golden silky path,
unnoticed. Neither spoke, but the sense of homecoming
curled around him. Love that would last danced in the sunlight shafting onto the bare floor, and in Adam's slow
stroke on her hair, her hand smoothing his chest. "We need

the kitchen up and running right away. I want to fill that lovely old pantry. We'll need an office, of course. I don't think I'll paint the house I rented. There can't be much to home-owning. I think I'll paint this one."

"Do you, love?" Adam reached lazily for a remote control lying on the windowsill. He pressed a button and used the guiding stick, and from the shadows, Nancy the Flatbed Hauler purred toward them.

Adam took the velvet box from Nancy's back and removed the engagement ring, showing Jillian the wedding band of diamonds. He removed the silver ring, replacing it with the wedding set. "They belong there. You have my heart—will you take my name?"

Modern convention said she could keep her name, but Adam's was her choice. "I love you, Adam," Jillian said unevenly. She couldn't speak, her heart too full for words.

"And I love you. I always will."

July filled Tallchief Mountain with wildflowers, daisies spreading across the highland meadow. The traditional bridal tepee of the Tallchiefs gleamed pale in the setting sun as Adam waited for his bride.

They'd come so far, crossing from a boy and a girl and trouble into a new life as a man and a woman. She brought him a softness and a joy he never thought possible, an easy, genteel, graceful way of handling the emotional moments as the men came to see him.

Adam smiled and watched the sunset spread over the crests of the rugged mountains. But then, Jillian wasn't always a lady. Sometimes she was a laughing girl, teasing him, making him feel young and carefree. At other times, she was a woman boldly taking what she wanted and then at other times, Adam enjoyed the flirtation, that cocky, sultry, come-with-me-big-boy look over her shoulder, her hips swaying as she climbed the stairs. Other times, as they worked on the house, making it comfortable for their new life, she was fierce, arguing with him.

When she was most frustrated, Adam greedily anticipated her next move, because it was likely she would leap
upon him, having her way to both their pleasures and sometimes in laughter and flirtation. And there was nothing like
her surging out of bed, stalking through the room, curved
and beautiful and itemizing exactly why she was right and
he was wrong. Nothing could compare to Jillian walking
to him at their wedding, dressed in a doeskin shift of the
Tallchiefs. Her amber eyes had darkened and shimmered
with tears as she took in his plaid and kilt, and the love he
could not keep from shining.

Jillian needed him, he thought, dazzled by the life open-
ing up in front of him. She needed him to listen to her
business complaints, to give comfort as she told him about
rebuilding her life, to listen to the wedding plans and those
of her garden. *She needed him for back rubs, which usually
developed into his appreciation for her body and his need
for it. She needed and loved him. His life was more than
he could have ever dreamed, more full.*

He picked a bouquet of wildflowers, thinking of how
tender she could be, how demanding a lover, sometimes
shocking herself. There were times when she looked across
a crowded room at him and the sizzle fairly undid him,
hardening him until he couldn't think of anything but how
she felt in his arms.

Adam shook his head and brought the bouquet to his
face, smelling it. True, he could be rude, packing her over
his shoulder and carrying her out of a family gathering to
have her alone.

He looked up at the mountain peaks where Liam had
chased Elizabeth, and knew he would have done the same.
And then he smiled, wondering who had really caught
whom. He wondered if Sarah knew all those years ago that
there would never be another love for him, that Jillian had
captured his young heart fast and tight.

Then Jillian stood away from the bush concealing the
small pool where they would bathe together later. She wore

his wedding ring, the headband of beads and doeskin, and nothing else. The sunset slid along her hair, burnishing it, and curving like a gold wrap along her body.

Adam watched, his throat dry and his heart beating heavily, as she walked toward him, the dove and the hawk feathers held in her outstretched hand, and love shining in those soft gold eyes.

"I know, dear heart. You don't have to say anything. It's in your face, and probably in mine. I feel just the same, loving you," she whispered as she smoothed his cheek.

"It's been forever. It will be forever, my love for you," he whispered, his voice raw, as he brought her palm to his lips.

The woman who brings the hawk and the dove feathers to the hunter shall tame him in gentler ways. He will be her strength, protecting her, but she has her own powers, most tender and loving.... Together they grow into each other's lives, and love will be born....

* * * * *

Don't miss

MR. TEMPTATION,

the launch title for Cait London's sizzling new miniseries,

HEARTBREAKERS,

which features heroes to die for, and the women they come to love.
On sale April 2002 from Silhouette Desire.

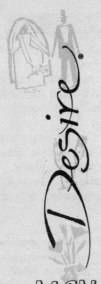

January 2002
THE REDEMPTION
OF JEFFERSON CADE
#1411 by BJ James

Don't miss the fifth
book in BJ James'
exciting miniseries
featuring irresistible
heroes from Belle Terre,
South Carolina.

M E N of Belle Terre

February 2002
THE PLAYBOY SHEIKH
#1417 by Alexandra Sellers

Alexandra Sellers
continues her sensual
miniseries about
powerful sheikhs
and the women
they're destined
to love.

SONS OF THE DESERT

March 2002
BILLIONAIRE
BACHELORS: STONE
#1423 by Anne Marie Winston

Bestselling author
Anne Marie Winston's
Billionaire Bachelors prove they're
not immune to the power of love.

MAN OF THE MONTH

Some men are made for lovin'—and you're sure to love
these three upcoming men of the month!

Available at your favorite retail outlet.

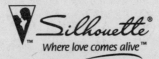

Silhouette®

Where love comes alive™

Visit Silhouette at www.eHarlequin.com

SDMOM02Q1

You are invited to enter the exclusive, masculine world of the...

TEXAS Cattleman's Club
The Last Bachelor!

Silhouette Desire's powerful miniseries features five wealthy Texas bachelors—all members of the state's most prestigious club—who set out to uncover a traitor in their midst... and discover their true loves!

THE MILLIONAIRE'S PREGNANT BRIDE
by Dixie Browning
February 2002 (SD #1420)

HER LONE STAR PROTECTOR
by Peggy Moreland
March 2002 (SD #1426)

TALL, DARK...AND FRAMED?
by Cathleen Galitz
April 2002 (SD #1433)

THE PLAYBOY MEETS HIS MATCH
by Sara Orwig
May 2002 (SD #1438)

THE BACHELOR TAKES A WIFE
by Jackie Merritt
June 2002 (SD #1444)

Available at your favorite retail outlet.

Silhouette®
Where love comes alive™

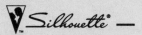

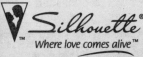

If you enjoyed what you just read,
then we've got an offer you can't resist!

Take 2 bestselling
love stories FREE!

Plus get a FREE surprise gift!

Clip this page and mail it to Silhouette Reader Service™

IN U.S.A.
3010 Walden Ave.
P.O. Box 1867
Buffalo, N.Y. 14240-1867

IN CANADA
P.O. Box 609
Fort Erie, Ontario
L2A 5X3

YES! Please send me 2 free Silhouette Desire® novels and my free surprise gift. After receiving them, if I don't wish to receive anymore, I can return the shipping statement marked cancel. If I don't cancel, I will receive 6 brand-new novels every month, before they're available in stores! In the U.S.A., bill me at the bargain price of $3.34 plus 25¢ shipping and handling per book and applicable sales tax, if any*. In Canada, bill me at the bargain price of $3.74 plus 25¢ shipping and handling per book and applicable taxes**. That's the complete price and a savings of at least 10% off the cover prices—what a great deal! I understand that accepting the 2 free books and gift places me under no obligation ever to buy any books. I can always return a shipment and cancel at any time. Even if I never buy another book from Silhouette, the 2 free books and gift are mine to keep forever.

225 SEN DFNS
326 SEN DFNT

Name _____ (PLEASE PRINT)

Address _____ Apt.# _____

City _____ State/Prov. _____ Zip/Postal Code _____

* Terms and prices subject to change without notice. Sales tax applicable in N.Y.
** Canadian residents will be charged applicable provincial taxes and GST.
  All orders subject to approval. Offer limited to one per household and not valid to
  current Silhouette Desire® subscribers.
® are registered trademarks of Harlequin Enterprises Limited.

DES01   ©1998 Harlequin Enterprises Limited

Silhouette® Desire®

presents

DYNASTIES: THE CONNELLYS

A brand-new miniseries about the Connellys of Chicago,
a wealthy, powerful American family tied by blood to the
royal family of the island kingdom of Altaria.
They're wealthy, powerful and rocked by
scandal, betrayal…and passion!

Look for a whole year of glamorous and
utterly romantic tales in 2002:

January: **TALL, DARK & ROYAL by Leanne Banks**

February: **MATERNALLY YOURS by Kathie DeNosky**

March: **THE SHEIKH TAKES A BRIDE by Caroline Cross**

April: **THE SEAL'S SURRENDER by Maureen Child**

May: **PLAIN JANE & DOCTOR DAD by Kate Little**

June: **AND THE WINNER GETS…MARRIED! by Metsy Hingle**

July: **THE ROYAL & THE RUNAWAY BRIDE by Kathryn Jensen**

August: **HIS E-MAIL ORDER WIFE by Kristi Gold**

September: **THE SECRET BABY BOND by Cindy Gerard**

October: **CINDERELLA'S CONVENIENT HUSBAND
by Katherine Garbera**

November: **EXPECTING…AND IN DANGER by Eileen Wilks**

December: **CHEROKEE MARRIAGE DARE
by Sheri WhiteFeather**

Silhouette®

Where love comes alive™